Having served a brief term in the military gave Kina the start for her training as a better-than-average pilot of large spaceships. Using that training to give her a jump in her career, she lands a job in one of the system's best passenger and freight companies. It doesn't take her long to move up to one of the supreme spots as captain of the best passenger liners going from the busy civilized worlds. Kina and her crew thought she had it made until a stalker began to show up wherever her ship was docked.

Because that put her crew and passengers in danger, the company moved her over to a different division hauling freight. But nothing could catch or halt the large mysterious figure who was ruining her life.

What was worse, he began to put thoughts in her mind that there might be a better life for her out in dark space—one where her life wasn't run by the rules of a corporation but where she might be free on her ship. What was the secret this stalker knew that she needed to discover?

Dark Space Secrets

ISBN: 978-1-4874-3920-0
Cover art by Martine Jardin

Published by eXtasy Books Inc

Look for us online at:
www.eXtasybooks.com

Dark Space Secrets

By

M. Garnet

Dedication

I need to say thanks to my Thursday night Zoom group Fan the Flame. Every meeting we bounce ideas off each other and they helped me with the strange title of this novel. Thanks all you great gals!

Chapter One

Captain Kina Russel knew she was being followed. She was on her way to work, and on purpose she'd taken a long way down the back halls of the shopping area. The company ships were docked at satellite stations for standard routes over busy commercial planets.

Many corporations had spaceships flying the standard routes for the many heavily colonized planets among these nearby systems. The different companies all hauled visitors, businesspeople, and supplies of all sizes.

The ship that Kina flew was a good one, not the newest, but a fast one, kept in top condition, and mainly handled people. It had a couple of small bays for reasonable supplies. It always brought in extra funds for the company to put something in the bays.

All clothing that the employees of Shayde Transport, Inc. wore was in different tones of purple. The large ship had the trademark name in large letters on both sides of the nose in deep purple. Kina's uniform as an officer was dark purple, and she wore a one-piece suit under a jacket of the same color. The jacket had all the fancy buttons and epaulets befitting her rank, in addition to emblems on the sleeves.

Pulling up her pad, she opened it and set it as if to take a picture of herself. This allowed her to see behind without turning around or glancing over her shoulder. Just coming into the dark hall, outlined by the light from the grand walkway, was the tall figure.

Frustrated, Kina turned off her pad, grasped it tight as she turned, and began running back.

"Hey, what do you want?" But before she had taken several steps, the tall, dark shadow was back out and around the corner. It or he was gone. When she reached the wide corridor, there was only the usual traffic and no unusually tall person in dark clothes.

Damn. She had hoped to approach him at least once to find out what this whole thing was all about. Having this shadow behind her, no matter where she went, was beginning to wear thin on her nerves. She was proud of her nerves, as they had gotten her to the position of *Pilot* on the ship *Ascher Shayde.* The line was long and cutthroat for a position as a pilot on any of the big corporation travel ships.

Even being top of her class did not count, as it the position required two years of pilot service for the Federated Union. A special Badge of Courage was what had probably topped off her resume. Bravery was not a problem for Kina, but to have a significant question unanswered was like a sore tooth that couldn't be treated.

Kina had not cheated. She had started at the bottom in the Shayde transport group, flying short hops as single or co-pilot with old ships from odd ports to stops right down on planets. But she played by the rules and did extra work, volunteering for trips no one else wanted. Kina spent more hours on the bridge than was required and slowly worked her way up, quicker than most. Okay, being an attractive woman, she might have added some special treats to get some recommendations. Her thought was to use what you had, and her talent behind the navigation bridge was great, but if a trip to a bunk helped, well, that was useful.

Months before, the hair on the back of her neck had begun to stand up when she saw precisely the same tall figure wherever she went off the ship. Kina never saw a face, as there was always a hood from a cape or a heavy cap pulled low and sometimes a breathing mask. But the shape was the same, about six foot four, broad shoulders, strong and fast moving.

It reminded her of the assassins she had read about in her romance books, but he had plenty of time to kill her. He merely followed her or stood outside her assigned room.

The police had been useless since she was in so many different locations. The first group of the local police had asked many questions that she mostly had negative answers to. He wasn't always there and never in the same place. She didn't have any enemies and did not have a job that led to secrets or danger. They promised to keep an eye on her while she was at their location.

Making a report to the Security of the Shayde Corporation had the same results. Did she have any old boyfriends? Maybe her family was checking on her. She explained she was an orphan and her boyfriends were now flying for the same company.

She hit her emergency comm button the next time she saw him in a crowd of passengers getting ready to board her ship, but he disappeared before security arrived. She apologized and gave up on outside help. She was going to have to trap her stalker somehow and get some answers. Her nerves were beginning to show as she drank too much coffee on the bridge.

The hostess in the light purple dress had suggested that she bring Kina some tea or decaf coffee. But Kina barked at the woman and had several cups of the straight black stuff before she remembered to apologize to the hostess. It wasn't the woman's fault. It was a big guy following her on every satellite that they nosed the big ship into the dock.

Sitting at her dashboard, she looked over at the second pilot, who was assisting and communicating with the satellite's control system. A thought suddenly hit her. How did her stalker get to all the systems that she traveled to each time she landed?

"Sha One, how many people did we carry this time?"

Sha One was the name of their AI that helped run things on the ship.

"Captain Russel, we carried two hundred and five passengers."

Punching some general buttons to complete the shutdown, Kina spoke again. "And Sha One, how many crew was on board this trip?"

"Captain Russel, we have the normal crew complement of one hundred twelve." Kina hit the last button and sat back. "So, Sha One, when we landed before anyone exited the ship, we had exactly three hundred and seventeen people on board the ship. Is that correct?"

The other pilot finished his job and nodded, and also sat back. They had to wait a few minutes before leaving their position.

The AI said, "No, Captain Russel. Before anyone departed, there were exactly three hundred and eighteen people on board the ship."

Captain Yari Dru, who had started to rise from his position, froze for a second and then turned to hit a minor alarm. He was the one to give the next orders. "Sha One, lock down the ship. Order the crew at the two exits back inside and notify Shayde Security at this location. Also, notify the local security staff. We need to review any cameras, both on our ship and the loading dock, for face recognition." He sank back into his seat and looked at his partner. "We had a stowaway on board."

While they waited for all the law officers to show up, the two pilots had the AI run a face ID on all the crew. Everyone was approved, so the stowaway had left the ship with the passengers.

All the passengers had ID shots on file when entering the

ship, so the one person who had left that would not match the files would be the one the law would be looking for on the space station.

After a few hours and too much coffee, Kina was frustrated. She was sure she had discovered how her stalker had followed her through so many places. She also felt he would at least be identified in a video. But there was no trace of any unidentified person on any of the many cameras, both in the door locks of the ship, on the outside of the ship, and especially in the large docking areas.

In the main galley of the ship *Ascher Shayde,* there was a crowd of law officers with various types of equipment. The Shayde Security people came with technical help and True Security with the capital on their name. These people wore side arms and asked brief questions with never a smile.

Between the use of the ship's AI and what they could see on all the cameras, making a comparison of all known faces attached to the ship and known workers to the dock, they had nothing. There was no trace of an extra person leaving the ship, nor was there any stowaway left on board.

Sitting in a corner of the galley, sipping another hot cup of what she knew she shouldn't be drinking, Kina kept her anger inside. He had done it again. She now understood how he had always appeared in all the places she traveled. *He had been on board her ship.* But he was like an invisible wraith, never being caught on any vid, camera or sensor. That was impossible because she knew he was alive and always there. She also believed she was not insane—she did have a follower, but why?

Thinking about her life and her job, she found nothing that would draw special attention. She didn't have a job that led to special intelligence or top secrets. Their corporation ship was only a means of transport for public use on standard routes. Her love life had been boring, with only a couple of flings and a few one-nights in between her hard work and many studies. She'd had opportunities that she had refused due to her schedule.

Taking a deep gulp and listening to the locals as they were wrapping up, she knew someone was watching her but still didn't know who or why. Finally, she listened to what was being said.

"We will need some time to do an in-depth search on all the dock cameras. A person could be hidden among the passengers or workers, and it will take hours to backtrack on each face." The announcement was made by an officer in a local law uniform with some braid on his shoulders. "But we need to go back to our own offices with larger mainframes and make a broader study."

This meant that most of the people were leaving the ship. It still took everyone a bit for the crowd to leave, which left the two captains with the local Shayde Security. It was quiet on the ship with the crew locked in Bay One and the captains in the main galley with company security with both groups.

"Stowaways try to get on all passenger ships all the time." It was the lieutenant in charge of the security detail with the two captains. He was helping himself to a mug of fresh coffee. All the machines were automatic to give service to passengers, and the products were tops. It was obvious he enjoyed the taste of the better coffee on board her ship.

Leaning his hips against the counter, he looked at his team and the two people who piloted this ship. "Sha One, when did you discover an additional person on board this ship?"

"Security Lieutenant Rever. It was when Captain Russel requested a head count at the dock as everyone was debarking." The emotionless voice of the AI would only respond to a question without adding any additional details. The LT. sighed, as he knew it would take a lot of simple questions to get all the answers, and he might never get the answers he needed.

Lt. River looked at the two people in the room responsible

for the big spaceship. "Who asked for a head count?"

"I did," Kina responded over her mug.

The tall lieutenant was good at his job. Kina had been watching him, and she had decided that he had to be previous military, probably Space Marine. This particular satellite was large and located over a bustling planet. The planet was a true Goldilocks find and had been colonized for centuries.

Better still, it had a large amount of land located in a great climate area along large oceans. This had immediately developed into a place to draw crowds and vacationers. It also drew casinos and lots of water sports. It was an important place for all the passenger ships to disembark and pick up passengers. That made it essential to the home office of Shayde Transportation.

The lieutenant turned toward Kina, and she was now on the hot seat. How did she explain this without sounding like an idiot and being put on hold in her job?

Chapter Two

Taking a deep breath, she decided to try for the corporate side. "It seemed like the passengers were slowly disembarking. I decided that a normal head count would explain some of the problems. It is standard in the Shayde manual."

Still in the relaxed position against the cabinet, the lieutenant set down his mug and pulled out and expanded a military pad. "You filed a report to different officials about a stalker. Did this headcount have anything to do with that report?"

Looking the security man directly in the eyes, Kina spoke clearly and firmly. "No one has been able to confirm my accusations. That problem is still an open question."

Still scanning his pad, the LT. asked, "Any proof of your feelings?"

With a deep sigh, Kina pulled out her private comm unit, a small individual unit, and brought up a small floating screen. After only a couple of scans, she brought up a view of the shadow at the end of the alley. Next, she showed the same shape in a dock, again the same shape in a doorway. She stopped after six others., waiting for the lieutenant to comment.

"An old lover?" His question was in a low voice as he took time to look at her closely.

"I wish."

The security man was frowning at her and then looked again at his pad, hidden from their view. At last he spoke without lifting his head. "The company has rules about the private lives of employees interfering with their jobs."

Now Yari said with a touch of anger in his voice, "That refers to the actions of the employee." He had worked with Kina for over a year, and they were beginning to be a competent pair on the bridge, taking turns and helping in the docking or loading. He had a lot of respect for her and liked her. "What she has reported is outside interference. It does not interfere with her performance. She is one of the best, if not *the* best, pilots Shayde has in their stable." He ended that with a nod.

"Perhaps." The lieutenant had a look of study on his strong face. This was a man who was always looking for problems and was on guard. His following command to the ship's AI was a report that the entire crew had been confirmed as present, and DNA tests proved positive.

"It seems our stowaway is now in the hands of the station law officials." The lieutenant shut his pad down and stood up. "I'm going to release the crew and let the locals chase this shadow down. But I do suggest that for the loading and the next couple of trips, we are going to put a closer check on all crew and passengers. We will make sure we don't allow any more free rides on this ship in the future." With these words, he left the room, taking a group of security people with him.

The two captains sat there in silence as they heard the heavy boots tromping down the hallway. Then, at last, Yari broke out laughing. "That guy thinks he's still in the Space Service. What a hard ass."

"Yari." Kina reached over and grabbed her friend's hand. "Thank you for speaking up for me."

"No. I meant every word. That guy is looking at us and not at the stowaway. Damn idiot." He got up and refilled his mug, then turned and reached for hers. She waved him off, knowing her bladder was floating and she needed to hit the head.

"Let me make a quick stop, and we can check everything out before the release crew takes over cleaning up. I think I need to get away for a while." She headed out of the wide doors, not sure if she was relieved or not. Was the security guy going to look into her stalker problem or drop the whole incident? One thing was good about the whole stowaway event. Their ship was going to have better checks on everyone entering the ship for the next few trips, and that would make her stalker have to take a different way to keep up with her.

After she and Yari double-checked everything on the bridge, including the final logs and one last exchange with station control, they were done for two days. During that time, the ship would be cleaned, minor repairs done, cartons removed, and new ones loaded into the bays.

Since there was no crew change at this stop, everyone had two days off and would report back on time. The pay was good for corporate work. The benefits were okay, and no one would miss the next load time for employment at Shayde.

The problem Kina had was she didn't want to stay on the station when she believed her stalker was wandering around and watching her. She decided to take a trip down to the planet. Since this was a visitor's paradise, the shuttle service ran continuously and was free with a tip to the driver and hostess. All anyone had to do was go to the nearest exit that had so many signs, and there were many exits available. With a small tote on one shoulder, Kina was soon in a comfortable seat with many happy travelers and a couple of businesspeople.

The businesspeople and Kina were the only ones not accepting drinks and laughing so much, as the rest were already having a good time. What she wanted to find was a quiet chair under a wide tree in the shade where she could read a story on her special private comm. The private one she had was commonly called a Review and could hold tons of books and movies and connect with local news as well as universal media. She wanted to get lost in someone else's life and forget about her problems.

Once on the ground and with the help of a friendly driver, it took her about two hours to stand at the front desk of a small hotel. With all the rooms on ground level, she was soon out of her uniform clothes and into a skimpy sundress. At the suggestion of a waitress, she was where she wanted to be, in a long low seat under an umbrella and watching the waves on the beach. The beach was a long walk away, and she hardly heard the children laughing and running. It was perfect, and she found herself leaning back and closing her eyes.

It was the shadow of a man falling over her that made her tense up as Kina gathered her muscles. If this turned out to be her stalker, he would find her ready to fight.

"Can I bring you something from the bar, Miss?"

Opening her eyes, Kina was looking at a waiter dressed in a swimsuit and a bow tie and nothing else. It was an interesting and enticing costume, but she was too uptight to appreciate the handsome man. Shaking her head, she dismissed him with a wave. As she watched him walk away, she shook herself. She couldn't even relax and enjoy a friendly local server. This whole thing was ridiculous.

Deciding this was a waste of time, she returned to her room and changed to return to the satellite and her cabin on the *Ascher Shayde*. The cleaning bots and some service people were still on the ship, but her cabin was finished, so no one would disturb her. Kina finally relaxed on her bunk, not even taking off her boots. She thought about the extra steps that company security was putting in place. Due to the stowaway, there was going to be closer scrutiny of all passengers and crew as everyone boarded from now on for further travel. Her stalker would have to find another way to get to the places where she was posted to follow her. Maybe he would even stop if it became too difficult and expensive for space travel.

Yari returned, and soon they fell into a normal routine of getting the ship ready for the next trip. Boarding was a little slower due to the new facial ID at each of the two main door locks. Fortunately, with complimentary hor d'oeuvres and drinks waiting inside, there were few complaints.

The ship had a routine route that took two months to complete, going through several jump gates to reach locations on heavily populated worlds. On each of the following stops, Kina elected to stay with the ship, avoiding any contact with locals. At last they made the final trip that brought them back to the large docking area at a satellite over the planet Solcap II.

This was the home of the Shayde Corporation and where Kina Russel had been born. Or at least it was put on her birth certificate, since she had been found as a baby abandoned and, it was assumed, left by a local teenage mother in the area. There were never any results from the DNA search, so the mother must have at least stayed out of trouble. Also, there was no family trace through the broad path of DNA for familial search either. That meant the father had either stayed out of reach of law or never been in the service.

DNA testing and the storage of the results with sharing was standard procedure. For example, all employees of transport companies had their DNA on registration. Kina had a few old friends from this home world, but like her, they all traveled or worked on different worlds. It was rare to get together, so she had no reason to look forward to going down for a visit.

As they were finishing up, Yari reminded her of the corporate party. Each time a corporate ship returned from full swing, there was a company party. It was on the planet in the lobby of the large building that housed the residents of Shayde. It was a bore, as the lower ranking crew and general workers at the corporate office drank too much. All the prominent officials and any ship officers would only take enough to be polite and slip out early, right after the top CEO made a speech on a vid. The lady CEO never made a personal appearance.

"Sha One, is the crew shuttle ready?" Yari was setting the ship up for the cleaning and repair crews as usual. Under the new security setup, either captain gave the AI a final check of people on board.

"Captain Dru," the AI said on the monotone. "The shuttle is ready in Bay One, and all crew is now boarding at that location. You two are the last on board."

Nodding, Yari, who was already standing, waved Kina ahead of him as he spoke one last time for the previous formal report. "Fine, Sha One. Give me the final count of the entire crew for security report."

"Entire count of all crew aboard is one hundred eleven. The shuttle is run by an AI pilot. Have a nice trip."

They both were several steps toward the door lock off the bridge when the words of the count hit both of them. The eyes of both captains met as they turned to look at the large dashboard.

Not saying anything, Kina looked at what she was used to calling her home and waited. It was Yari who finally walked back to put his hands on the dashboard and speak to the AI.

"Sha One, please confirm the correct number of humans now onboard spaceship *Ascher Shayde.*"

"Captain Dru, including the two captains on the bridge, there are one hundred eleven humans, all of their crew, on board this ship." The voice was always on the same level with no change.

"Sha One." Yari's voice was a bit loud and tense. "When we left our last port, I remember you reported that we had a crew contingency of one hundred twelve. Was that report correct?"

"Yes, Captain Dru. I cannot make a mistake on counts and in answers to your direct questions. It is how I am programmed."

Kina moved up next to Yari and looked out at the busy docking area through the wide front window over the dashboard. She also glanced up at a couple of screens that were still active and showed the outside where the passengers had embarked, but those doors had been closed.

Chapter Three

This time they had a more prominent security force on board, with a large local law department on the outside, blocking off the area around their docking site. There were also Shayde Security people among the law force surrounding all the docking sites.

Everyone, including the two captains, was taken down under tight escort to the planet. They were all separated and kept in comfortable but confined rooms in a building next to the large corporate structure.

A simple but adequate meal was served to Kina, and she assumed it was the same one given to everyone on the two floors of the structure. It was handed in through the door by a security guard who did not speak.

Right after the meal, Kina had her first visitor, and it was the same security guard who had brought the meal.

His words were brief. "Please follow me and do not speak."

Kina was led on a private elevator to a room in the basement and went through her first interrogation. It was a simple question and answer that she felt she could be truthful about. This first session was all about the crew and when and where she had seen any of them.

Since she also wanted information on the missing ship worker, she took all the questions seriously and even took a bit of time to answer some. She felt she needed to think about some instances of when she had moved through the ship. Instances when she had made standard trips for inspections and contacts. Then there were others when she was only wandering.

Four machines in the room were monitoring her as she spoke. Kina was familiar with the units, as she had to pass such tests to become a pilot. They checked her body movements, body heat, blood pressure, heartbeat, and brain response. The machines were making sure she told the truth or standard lie detectors.

Being escorted back to her room, Kina did notice that the security people were careful that she never passed anyone in the halls. They were keeping everyone separated to find out who was the last person to see the missing crew person and find out when he became missing.

The crew was kept in isolation for two nights and three days. Under normal circumstances, this would be illegal, but it was all covered in the contract they had all signed when they hired on with the Shayde Corporation. On the third day, Kina followed a security guard down to a floor that surprised her. This time it wasn't the basement—it was on the first floor.

As they walked across a large lobby with ordinary people moving around, she saw other members of her crew following security people. They all ended up in an auditorium.

Everyone settled down. Kina soon found Yari, and they took seats near the front but at one side. One hundred and eleven people, some angry but most confused, sat down in their freshly cleaned uniforms. They all got quiet as a couple of men in dark civilian suits made their way to the front.

A floating comm unit dropped down in front of one who was standing, and he looked around.

"By this time, you are all aware that we have had some stowaway incidents on our ships. It is something that plagues all of the normal transit companies. Unfortunately, our good ship *Ascher Shayde* has had some unusual events—stowaways that found a way to enter and leave that ship without leaving any trace. This especially disturbs us, not the fact of someone getting a free ride, but the fact that it puts the ship, its passengers, and the whole crew in danger."

He stopped and looked at the man at his side. These two were average men but had a serious look about them. They also wore very expensive suits and had a look of confidence. Kina had a feeling they were lawyers.

"This last incident is a point of interest. One of the crew members of the *Ascher Shayde,* a Junior Engineer Assistant by the name of Del Kimp, was found in a cheap overnight sleep room on satellite Mazon. That was one of your standard stops for your route on the passenger ship. At that point, the AI on the ship reported all crew personnel present and continued to report full until you docked at here, the home depot."

The solemn words brought out some small mutters among the people sitting in the room. It finally dawned on several among them that they had been working, sleeping, and eating with a stranger.

The man continued in his firm manner. "The good news is that Mr. Kimp is in good condition. He had been drugged, and, upon awaking, reported to one of our offices. The Corporation staff, along with the Head of Security, has made a decision. First, the *Ascher Shayde* is being pulled out of service for some new upgrades. Next, all of you will be assigned to new positions, equal to what you did on the *Ascher Shayde* but not together. It is the thought of security to protect all of you from what happened to Mr. Kimp. If you are separated and put with other crews, it will protect you and the passengers of Shayde Transport."

While everyone sat in shocked silence, realizing they were going to lose some good friendships, the second man stepped forward. "Okay, folks. This has been tough on all of us. You all have a few days off. Relax and enjoy what the city has to offer. The standard service rooms are waiting for you at the hotel, and transportation is out in front. At this time, we are not going to answer any questions."

With these words, everyone could hear large doors opening behind them. The two men walked off, surrounded by security staff.

"So they are breaking us up," Yari said in a low voice so that only Kina heard him as they walked through the crowd to the floating buses.

Pulling on his arm, she dragged them off to one side at the edge of the street. "Yari, he was with me on the ship all the time. What does he want?"

"Easy, girl." Yari reached out and put an arm around her shoulder. "You don't even know who was on the ship. The security people will search through all the cameras, and they will find a vid of our extra crewman. No one can hide forever from Sha One."

"But who is he? Why is he following me and taking these great risks?" Kina let the anger come through as she spoke to her friend. "Damn, Yari. I'm going to miss you."

"Yeah, this breakup of the crew sucks. We did make a great team on the bridge. Look, once we get our new assignments, we need to make sure to get together on docking stops. Let's plan ahead as soon as possible." Now, he turned them both to start toward the buses.

By the time they all were transported to the standard employee hotel that was reserved for Shayde personnel only, Kina was ready for a drink and a nap. Unfortunately, there was a screen open in her room. With a sigh as she entered the room, expecting to see her tote in place from the ship, she went over to the screen and accepted the notice.

It was from Security, setting her up with an appointment for the next morning. Well, at least she would have time for a long shower, a good meal, and a long rest. Kina sent a notice to Yari that she would see him the next day after a meeting with Security, and while the screen was open, she ordered a meal.

After a restless night, Kina was grateful that her appointment with Security was early and in the same building, just on the first floor. Her usual breakfast of coffee did not help her stomach as she looked out the large window. As a captain, she had a nicer room that had a large wall that was mostly window, looking down on the busy street.

Finally she made her way down to her appointment. She had some dread and some hope. No one ever wanted meetings with security, but maybe there was a chance that they had found some trace of the stowaway on the ship.

It seemed like everyone in security was trained never to smile. A permanent impassive look was pasted on the face of every person inside the offices as Kina entered the marked door on the first floor. This was a primary setup for the local division of Shayde's Security. That made sense, since the hotel seemed to be owned by the same company and was not open to the public.

A female guard sitting behind a desk looked up as Kina entered and nodded without a smile. "Can I help you?"

"I'm Captain Russel. I was told that I had an appointment this morning."

The guard glanced at a screen that had the back covered so that it could only be viewed by her, looked at it, and then nodded. "Yes, go through the door on the left, which is the second door. It will be open." The guard turned back to entering items into a keyboard.

Looking around, Kina walked over to the indicated door, opened it, and found herself in a long hallway with people moving from room to room. All of the doors, as far as she could see, were open, and when she went past the first one, people were moving around cabinets, with one behind a desk.

Everyone seemed busy. The second door opened into an office with an officer who had his back turned as he was working on a screen and equipment on the wall.

Knocking on the open door, she only took one step inside and waited.

The man glanced over his shoulder and turned. "Oh, Captain Russel, have a seat. I'll be right with you." With those words, he turned back to the wall and equipment and plugged in a couple of extra wires.

This was something that usually a tech would handle, but Kina sat down in the standard office chair and took advantage of the time to look at the officer.

This time the man was older, could be her father, but was obviously in shape under the tight shirt that stretched as he lifted his arms. At last, the man turned, pulled out a tall-backed chair, and sat down, sliding forward to let his arms fold up on the desk. He took a long moment to stare at her, then hit a couple of buttons that brought up a small privacy screen.

"Captain Russel, we have a problem."

This man's voice was a rich deep tenor that carried the tone of one used to giving orders. He had been around for a while, both in the military and in security for Shayde. Kina looked at his uniform, trying to decide if there was a grade on it, but there were no markings to show, even if he was an officer. Still, she knew he had to be high up in security.

At this point, and with the words he spoke, she felt that silence on her part was the best action. She waited to see what he might add to the conversation.

CHAPTER FOUR

"You have made things very complicated for Shayde Transports. Are you aware of that?"

He leaned forward. Kina realized there was no noise in the hallway behind her by the open door.

"I have to admit, Sir, that I don't understand the complication you are referring to." Kina was giving an honest answer and hoped it showed on her face.

He turned away from his screen and looked across the clean desk at her. "You are one of the finest pilots out in the deep dark. You were top of your grade in each enterprise and are top of the line in all reports for Shayde Transport. All those people who have worked with you have only given you high remarks. But…" Here, he hesitated and glanced at the hidden screen.

Kina straightened up and faced him. She knew what was coming. Some damn stalker was about to ruin her life.

"We can't keep risking passengers. It opens us up to lawsuits, but we also don't want to lose so much talent. We need to put you over into one of our other companies, one where your talent as a good pilot will be used and where no passengers will be at risk. We are transferring you to a different leg of our company."

With no time to say goodbye to anyone, Kina decided she would send Yari a note later. She was told to gather personal items from her room as she was being moved to a different location and would be issued different uniforms.

An airbus that was for general transportation for employees only was outside the hotel with the Shayde logo on it. Kina had been instructed to take it to the local train station, where she would travel almost halfway around the world to another Shayde depot.

First of all, unlike the landing zone for the passenger terminals, where there were only a few shuttles that came down from the docking satellite, all was clean and quiet, and moving sidewalks kept traffic in slow groups.

When Kina got off the train at Shayde Commodity Transportation, everything was chaos. Robot haulers were moving large crates in all directions, landing loads for large shuttles and tow ships. Kina found herself in a different world of Shayde Transport. Here, everyone was in clothes of brown, some light beige and some dark to almost black.

She could hear the continuous noise of the landing and the rising of vehicles. Following the old signs and faded yellow lines, Kina made her way to the control offices, where she was made to wait until an officer from out on the area that was covered in the strong thick material nicknamed crete was available to come in and take her upload from her wrist comm. As far as Kina could see, the crete spread out between large buildings with unusually wide-open doors.

She was in a different world from passenger transport. This area was for moving products from food to giant machinery around the many civilized worlds and beyond. It brought in as many funds, if not more, than the moving of people. But there was danger, as some items were expensive and had large insurance bonds involved. Others were dangerous because they were explosive or possibly flammable and needed special handling.

Finally, a man in a medium brown one-piece uniform came in and went immediately to the tall counter to pick up some flimsies. He turned, glanced at Kina, and nodded.

"So, you're our new hot-shot pilot. Great. Drop your info here."

He held out a portable scanner, and Kina hit her wrist comm and all her company info transferred. Then she realized he was moving out the door, so she hurried to follow before the door slammed in her face. He had a small personal floater waiting right in front of the walkway and was moving around it to get in the main seat. Taking the lead from him, she climbed into the seat beside him as she heard him giving the instructions to move. They were going off the side to an area of housing.

Everything was less formal and a bit impatient in this segment of the transportation line. The officer, who finally introduced himself as Major Brockman, instructed her to register for a room and request pilot uniforms to be sent to her room. He also said that a meeting for pilot assignments was every three hours, around the clock, in the main assembly room on the first floor of the hotel.

He took off so fast she felt a breeze as she stepped off the floater. The hotel she entered was entirely different from the one on the other side of the planet for pilots and crew. But the first thing she noticed was the Marines. They stood out in their camo uniforms. Evidently, due to transporting military items, the government was going to ensure that its presence was also felt.

She had a feeling of invulnerability having these large armed soldiers around. It would be hard for her stalker to make an appearance near here. Then there was the fact of so many people wearing different shades of brown, all in primarily one-piece uniforms.

The woman at the counter was quick and brisk. Kina obtained a room, and her uniforms were ordered. She was told there was no room service and the two cafeterias were open all the time with no special orders. Deciding that she needed to fit in as soon as possible, she changed into the comfortable dark brown uniform with the markings on the sleeves and collar. Then she went down to the first floor to find the meeting room and get her first assignment.

Since she was a pilot, she expected to be assigned to one of the ships docked up at the satellite that would be delivering goods to places that she had never visited. Well, perhaps she'd been to some of them, as all planets required food products and replacement parts for equipment.

She found the room as disorganized as the area outside, and she took a moment to step aside and look around. It had a few tables with chairs behind them along the back wall and down both sides. These were not neat or in rows, just haphazard, as if people pushed them aside as they moved around and no one straightened anything up afterward. A couple of men, behind a couple of the tables were looking upward.

Checking to see what they were examining, she saw a large screen up on the front wall. In some ways, it was like the destination board for many ships put up for passengers, so they'd know what time and which dock their ship was departing from.

But this one carried more information. It carried load weights, ship names, pilot names, first and second destinations, pilot upload time, departure time, and much more information. Major Brockman was standing at a large import station and seemed to be setting up more details on the display.

One of the men made a copy into his wrist comm by holding up his hand. He got up immediately and left the room, moving past Kina with only a nod at her. Deciding to take a seat and watch the action for a while, she moved to a chair apart from the other man. It wasn't long before a couple of other people entered together, one man and a woman. They moved together and sat at a table on the other side.

Glancing back up at the board, Kina was surprised to see her full name along the line with a lot of information. She had been assigned a ship. But at that moment, she heard the couple across the room talking.

"Look, they have the *Eclipse* back in action." It was the woman who drew her friend's attention to the board.

"Yes, I heard they had that old lady in for some great upgrades. That should be a great run. Too bad, I didn't get it." He leaned into the woman, and Kina couldn't hear the rest of what he was saying.

Getting her mind back on track, she punched a couple of times at her wrist comm, and some information from the board was downloaded. As she read the first lines, it seemed she had a ship to pilot, but she didn't have to report to a shuttle for six hours. This allowed her to eat and gather some personal things to take along. It also would allow her some time to get some information on the ship, the load, and the destination.

Her first stop was the store off the lobby of the hotel. These stores were standard in all hotels, and she wanted to fill out her personnel items and renew some things. With a couple of bags, she went to her room and had time to bring up information on the ship she would be handling. First, there was only general information about a large transport freighter built twenty years ago. But that was not the information Kina needed.

She logged in using her full name and title. She also pulled the first assigned numbers from the download from the Major's board. She now had a lot of information scrolling through the screen, so she had to slow it down and began to choose the index so she could control the information.

As captain, she was able to get the complete information on the *Eclipse Shayde* as it was now in Docking Station 12. This was nothing like the pretty, smooth passenger ships that Kina had piloted for the last two years. First, it was a monster, and there was nothing attractive about it, unless you preferred utilities.

The ship was a combination of black and non-reflective metal. The nose stuck out like a rod and was flanked on each side by two jutting matching rods that she would have to study later to find out their use. Perhaps they held equipment for deep navigation. This big ship docked sideways to unload large cargo, as well as having three-bay exits for shuttle departure. That explained why the ship was docked at Station 12. It was an extended docking site.

If the ship was huge, the engines were over the top. Four antimatter cores in the rear on each side and two additional steering engines on the side were larger than normal. This monster ship wasn't finished with surprises, as it carried a full load of weapons. The captain was assigned a Weapons Master for each delivery.

Sitting back with a frown, Kina realized they were not going to the pretty vacation planets. They must be making deliveries in rougher sites. Okay, there was a perk—the pay was higher for her. She wondered if it was for all the captains in this division of Shayde or just the captain of the *Eclipse*. It didn't matter, as she wasn't about to quit the company. The benefits and retirement package after fifteen years with the organization were good and worth struggling for. If they were able to find a place for someone who had personal problems, she was going to stay in any position they assigned to her. What did this all mean?

Chapter Five

An engineer who seemed to be in charge of the ship itself was the other crewman. The ship also was equipped with the standard AI that would help with navigation and had been upgraded to some type of military standards.

With a big ship and a large number of engines, Kina decided that she probably was going to have long runs and loaded her memory chips with a lot of reading material and some vids and movies. Later she would discover this had not been necessary. The ship's AI had a pleasant surprise for her once they were in the deep dark.

The information on the load that the ship was carrying was not listed, but the destination was open. The schedule would be three stops, a bit of a loop with offloading and loading that would bring them back home. It was a long trip in the star mileage, but the jumps would be easy with the engines on the *Eclipse*. Kina had never traveled to any of the indicated places, so she closed out the Shayde information site and did some research on the star grid.

Now, she began to understand why the ship had weapons. They were going beyond the regular civilized routes to the first planet called New Henry II. She had never heard of it, and there was little information on the media sites about the planet. It was just out off toward the fringe or past the busy areas where new worlds were being settled.

Deciding she couldn't learn much in the hotel room, Kina took a floater out and got the information and location for a shuttle up to the satellite. Getting up to the satellite from the busy area wasn't a problem for someone wearing the brown one-piece uniform of a captain. Her comm was checked, along with a swipe of DNA, and she was allowed to board the first shuttle she found that was open for passengers. Most of the shuttles would carry people up to the satellite and back down to her new area. Sometimes there was only a small room right behind the pilot's location.

Unfortunately, once up in the docking area reserved for this type of shipping, the only way of getting around was to walk. Walking meant avoiding the movers that constantly zipped by with different items on board, from crates to equipment. These were all run by their own AI systems. They did stop fast or turn around each other amazingly quickly, but it was a bit nerve-wracking for the humans. There was an orange line with lights to follow for bipeds, but it was crossed over by the movers when the units needed to get to another area.

To make the trip worse for Kina, her big ship was docked in the last slot. This meant a long walk, with a lot of ducking away from big moving crates. When she finally got near her ship, it was strangely a quiet area. Either it was already loaded, or all of the items needed to be aboard were being loaded on the other side through the big bay doors. This meant the back of the ship was either open to airless space or had the expensive shields that held the atmosphere in with the doors open. If that was the case, this was going to be an interesting ship to fly.

Walking up the ramp to enter the first big side door lock, she was stopped by a force field. A blue light came on, and Kina realized she was being scanned. Then a deep male voice spoke.

"Welcome aboard, Captain Russel."

Looking around, Kina knew she was alone in the large entrance and assumed someone was watching her through one of the cameras. "Thank you. Who has greeted me, and will I meet you on the bridge?"

"I am Mark One, your ship's AI. Yes, we will meet on the bridge or anywhere else on the ship for your convenience." The male voice had some sentient emotion and didn't sound like the normal flat-sounding AI metal voices that Kina was used to, so she was surprised. She smiled as she realized this was going to be a trip with many surprises.

"May I suggest you take the left small walkway toward the front? It can be confusing on such a large ship at first." The male voice was a bit distracting with its realism, but she appreciated the instructions, as she had hesitated in the big bay. It took her fifteen minutes to reach a narrow hallway that led past cabins and into the bridge.

Standing in the door lock for a moment to get herself oriented, Kina found she was looking at a very modern, unadorned bridge. The pilot's seat was in the middle and was a separate unit. Off to the left were a dashboard and an enclosed seat that must be for weapons control. Another seat and a dashboard were located on the right, but it was blank at this time. There were the usual tucked-up seats on the back wall for visitors. This was a small area for such a monstrous ship, but it looked efficient. Permanent screens were placed above, and she realized the view window that wrapped around the entire dashboard was clear metal.

"You will find that the seat adjusts automatically to fit you. Do you have any questions, Captain?"

Kina looked around for speakers, but the clean look of the cabin did not show any mounted grills on the walls or ceiling. "No. I came aboard early to get a chance to look around."

"A good captain is always first aboard."

The voice now came directly from the dashboard in front of the pilot's seat. Kina stepped forward and leaned against the seat.

"There is no report at this time, Captain."

Kina set down her small tote and slid into the seat that began to adjust to her as the AI continued to speak in that amazing-sounding human male voice.

"Most of our deliveries have been loaded, except for a last-minute small device. Engineers Blahx and Weaponeer Warvel will report in about two hours. The gentleman that followed you is still on the dock."

"What?" Kina jumped up and turned. "AI, notify security. That is an unidentified person who needs to be apprehended. Where is he? Can you show me his location on any camera?" She was yelling as she stumbled over her tote and tried to get out of the door lock of the bridge.

"At once, Captain."

With a loud sound and a shake of the ship, Kina realized the outside doors were being slammed shut.

"No, I need to get to him." It was fruitless, as it would take her too long to get to any exit from such an enormous ship. He would be long gone as usual, and she would not see his face. Maybe the ship had a vid of him. Perhaps the security staff had something on him.

At last, hanging onto the frames around the door lock on the bridge, Kina stopped and took a deep breath. She did have to wonder how the hell he'd been able to track her all the time. It dawned on her that she must have some type of signal on her or in her stuff.

Going back to the tipped-over tote, she opened it and dumped everything out on the floor. Kina sat down on the cold metal next to it and wanted to cry. How would she recognize a modern tracker in all of her stuff, including the new items that were still in their packaging?

"Mark One, have my items been delivered onboard yet?" Kina asked from her slumped position.

"No, Captain. It has not arrived. Do you wish me to check

on its delivery?"

"No." Kina shook her head. So, if there was a tracker, it wasn't in the items still in her previous things. "How good is the med system on this ship?"

"It was one of the upgrades. It is top military grade. It is only one level below us in the front of the ship."

Stuffing everything back into the tote, she followed the AI's easy instructions to get down to the med sector. The AI wasn't wrong about the med bay being in top gear. She saw two beds separated, two med pods, and a deep bath for complete repairs. Inside were several med bots, and when she entered, one approached.

"May we help you, Captain?"

"I think I have a tracker either in my things or on my body. I want a complete invasive search." Kina set the tote on one bed, walked over to a pod, and began to strip.

An hour later, as she got dressed, she got the bad news that though she was extremely healthy, there were no trackers anywhere near her or inside her.

When she returned to the bridge, she requested the AI to show her any vids of the person who had followed her from the dock to the edge of the ship. On a split screen, there were several views of the tall figure, and no matter which one she looked at, none showed a face. This guy was good when it came to avoiding cameras.

"Damn," Kina said out loud, talking to herself. "There never is much to tell about him."

"I can give you some information," The AI announced. It brought up one vid of the figure coming through a door into the docking area. "In this view, I can estimate the figure is six foot five inches tall and has a solid figure which would put it or him at approximately two hundred thirty pounds. His movement proves complete control of muscle control, so probably military training or an athlete. I would estimate this would be classified by law enforcement as a dangerous individual."

Chapter Six

To say that Kina was grateful that she did not have to leave the ship before take-off time would be an understatement. Her luggage was transferred from the hotel to the small but comfortable cabin on board.

"Captain, your two crew personnel are now coming aboard," the male voice of the AI announced in her cabin. Kina had taken some time to get acquainted with the brain that was going to help her control this massive freighter. To her surprise and a feeling of uncomfortable doubt, the improved AI had some personality. It told her it had named itself because nothing about Ecli One sounded acceptable.

While it instantly took any direct orders from her, it also did many exercises on its own to keep the ship running smoothly. When asked if it could give her a complete report on the ship from the temperature of each sector to load weights and fuel stock, Kina soon found she had to make sure she limited the information she asked for in her reports, or she got too much data. It became a waste of time, and she had to interrupt the AI's babble.

Hearing that she was going to have some live people on board the ship, Kina turned around and got out of the pilot's chair. "Mark One, could you please request that the crew please come to the bridge so that we could meet."

The man in charge of the weapons was not what Kina expected. She'd thought he would be a big gruff ex-military man. The thin man with a neat mustache and clean-cut clothes looked like an academy professor.

"You have to be the captain. I'm Deakon Warvel, your expert weapon chief. Is this your first time flying out to the fringe routes? If so, don't worry. I've made the trip many times." With that, he stepped in and looked around. "Well, well, they did what they promised. They seemed to have upgraded everything."

Before she could say anything, as the man was going over the dashboard by the weapons seat, a large attractive woman stood in the doorway grinning.

"Don't pay any attention to that idiot, Captain." The woman stepped forward with her hand out.

Kina shook it and nodded. "Well, it is always good to have a crew that likes their work. I guess that means you are the engineer."

"Yep, First Class Briget Blahx, and I had handled this freighter for a couple of years before they pulled it in for a refit. I will let you know how excited I am once I get back and check out to see what upgrades the landlubbers have performed."

Not being able to resist returning the smile of the big woman, Kina shrugged. "Well, I don't have anything to add as a newcomer, so I'll let you get to either your cabin or your favorite place and check things out to see what those so-called landlubbers did to your engines. We do have a schedule already, and Mark One has the navigation set. Let me know when you are all set to go."

"Sure will, Cap." The handsome woman hurried from the bridge.

Turning, Kina had nothing to do except take her seat, but she decided to go first to the galley for coffee. It was her lifeblood, and she felt she needed it now for this first step of her new life. Also was the fact that her damn stalker was still on her tail. This guy was better than the Special Ops Corp of the Military.

Sitting silently for a moment in the unusually comfortable pilot's seat, Kina had to wonder what she had done to deserve this type of stress and threat.

"Captain, the best next step is to make contact between your comm and me as the ship's AI. Do you require help for this first step?" Mark One spoke directly in front of her through a small speaker on her dashboard. That woke her up and snapped her out of her mind wandering.

"No, thank you. I have this." With that, she brought her wrist up, hit a couple of buttons on it, and reached forward to touch a lit panel. There was a small jolt of upload, and she felt contact. She suddenly had a lot more information about the big freighter than she had been thinking about before. This was an amazing ship, and it was going to be an adventure.

This ship was over twenty years old and had traveled out beyond the civilized worlds more times than Kina had ever dreamed about. The things it had seen and stored in its archives were beyond belief, and it had fought many successful battles. The facts were that people knew about the pirates and thieves out beyond where the law forces could safely patrol.

Now she let her eyes wander over to where Deak sat in the other chair. He had explained that he preferred the short version of his name, and she liked the friendly approach. After all, they would spend a lot of time together on the bridge. But later, she would learn he had another position on the ship to handle the weapons.

"Captain." Mark One spoke to her through her wrist comm privately. "Engineer Blahx gives her compliments and has all engines up and ready. I have the two steering jets on set, and you have contact now to satellite station control for departure."

"*Eclipse Shayde,* this is Shayde Satellite control. You have direct release. Good flight."

Clearing her throat, Kina made sure she spoke clearly,

hoping it was picked up. "Shayde Satellite control, thank you, and we are leaving ASAP. See you when we return. Thank you, *out*." With that, Kina reached forward and began to drift her left hand over several floating buttons. The vibration was felt in her feet on the floor, but not up through the amazing seat that was wrapped around her to hold her in place. It was such a deep soft wrap that even a complete accident that destroyed the whole bridge would keep her inside the seat. Of course, she would be dead from other damage and possible lack of air, depending on where the accident happened.

The freighter was soon off, away from the dock and heading for a jump area. It moved as smoothly, if not better, than the fancy passenger ship Kina had flown for the last two years. Their first destination was two ship days away, and after the first jump, Kina left the ship in charge of the AI and relaxed.

After taking time to get some good sleep and some decent meals, Kina was on her way down to visit the engineer when she poked her head into a side open door and saw some equipment and pads used for exercise. So the company wanted its people to stay in shape—good.

Finding the engineer on a break, eating a sandwich, and sitting on a small crate was a pleasant surprise.

"Can I enter your workplace, Engineer?" Kina asked calmly.

"Hey, Cap. Welcome to the heart of our ship." The tall handsome woman stood up and kicked out another small crate. "Join me." She sat back down comfortably. "By the way, the name my friends call me is Briget, and I hope we will be friends."

"Friends it is, Briget. So, how are the upgrades? Since I was never on the *Eclipse* before, I have no idea what they did to improve this monster." Kina looked around at the dark but clean area, full of sizable pipes and tubes running into a big round housing.

"Well," Briget said, still with her mouth full. "I've been flying with the freight division for ten years. I got three of those flights on this very ship before there was a disagreement with some borders in the Revine Line, which is way out in the fringe. This old lady took some damage but held her own and brought us all home."

Taking a moment to swallow from a mug, Briget looked around and smiled. "They took her out of service and assigned us to other ships. But I have to say they did a right good job on the Queen when they put in the upgrades. This old bitch will outrun anything except a full-size battle cruiser and give it a fun chase. The antimatter engines make the jumps seem like a kid jumping rope."

Briget stuffed the last of her sandwich into her mouth and seemed proud of what she had said.

"Ok, I'll take your word that this is all good. I always thought a jump engine was only a jump engine. But what do I know? I'm only a captain." Kina said this with a wave of her hands and a big smile.

"We are through the first jump and steady in space, Captain." It was that interesting male voice of Mark One, the ship's AI.

"That's an example." Briget nodded. Even as big as we are, we make it through a jump faster than even the smaller ships that are all engine."

"Captain." The AI interrupted again. Kina looked at her engineer with raised eyebrows.

"Report, please," Kina demanded.

"We have received some reports from home world. I am sorry to report that the person that seemed to be unidentified as your stalker was not captured by security. They also were unable to get any clear vids, as the cameras in the dock area ceased to work for a short time. They are investigating further."

"Damn!" Standing, Kina had lost her feeling of comfort on the ship with this small crew.

The tall woman also stood up. "Hey, if you have a problem, you can share."

"Thanks, maybe at another time. I think I'll head back up to the bridge, since we can talk to home base." If she thought the passenger ship was long, the walk from engineering to the bridge of the freighter was fifteen minutes of fast steps. She did allow herself to stop at the galley to fill a couple of mugs of coffee, but when she got to the front door lock, the small area was empty.

Deak had also gone off somewhere else on this ship, perhaps to his cabin or wherever else he found interesting, as there were a lot of choices. Okay, she could easily drink both mugs of coffee as she slid into her seat.

"Mark One, are there any other messages from the home world?"

"Negative, Captain." The male voice made even those two words have a lot of meaning.

The two days for their first delivery turned out to be without any incident as they headed past the busy routes. They were in a steady orbit around a standard planet called Locey Max, and there were large shuttles attached to their smaller bay in back. Unloading was done automatically with people in off-ship suits and large machines that moved between the crates and the shuttles.

Both Briget and Deak were in suits and were overseeing the process, making sure that only the correct items were selected and moved out of the bay. Kina watched the show from her seat on several screens supplied by the AI with cameras on the insides of the bay and outside of the ship. One thing was for sure. There were an unlimited number of views available to the AI, who gave the captain any information she requested.

From the time the first shuttle arrived with a proper ID that Mark One approved until the last crate was finally removed, it took a little over six standard ship hours.

As captain, she made certain the proper forms were filed electronically for both sides and sent the final information back to the home headquarters.

They closed up the ship, and she watched her two people carefully.

"Captain, I can observe our crew if you need to take a break now." It was Mark One speaking through the small speaker in front of her.

"No, I will wait and watch until both people are safe inside and out of the off-ship suits. I am the captain and responsible for the crew. Thank you." She watched as both her crew did some final prep work in the airless bay and also saw the big solid double doors begin to close. Finally, one after the other, the two bulky figures moved forward and through the inner door lock to the inside of the ship. They would only need a moment in the separate area inside for sufficient air to be pumped in, and they could remove their suits.

Once her crew was safe, she checked for their next destination, which was further off the beaten path. It was a station called Marheineke Two. It had a dangerous route warning, and Kina wasn't sure what that meant.

Chapter Seven

What Kina discovered, both from what Mark One informed her and what she learned from her comm screen about Marheineke, was that the route itself was where the danger lay. There had been numerous attacks against travelers, no matter which jump port was used in the star maps.

Coming out of the first jump with Deak in the seat beside her, Kina was on alert, as well as Mark One. But all was quiet, and the few hours it took to get to the next jump position saw nothing, not even another freighter. Making a series of short jumps was a decision to play it safe. This allowed the small crew to get rest and meals in between once they found themselves alone in systems.

The freighter cleared the jump, coming back into real space, having traveled many star miles in a blink, and there they were greeted. Alarms went off as Mark One observed the presence of another ship, too close for comfort.

"So, this bugger is waiting right outside the jump area. Fuck." It was Deak, who seemed to disappear while his seat pulled up around him. He was activating weapons.

"Mark One, bring up full shields and warn engineering. We need full steering power." Kina hit a button that dropped the floating buttons, preferring the hands-on touch when needing to make fast decisions.

"We're being hailed, Captain." Mark One spoke through her hair bob that she had inserted quickly.

"Put them through, showing only my face." Kina did not

want to give out any information about her ship, including the weapon section around Deak. Even while she answered the call, she still brought the steering engines around and was moving away from the other ship.

After a flicker, the face of an average-looking man, probably in mid-life, appeared on the screen at Kina's side on the dashboard. Kina took a second to copy a vid of him on her comm, even though she knew the ship's AI would be making a log archive.

Without voice on, she heard Deak mutter to her. "Doesn't look like a scary pirate. Looks like my dad's next-door neighbor."

"Yep," Kina agreed. "Never depend on stereotypes." She hit the button to accept the full call.

"Captain, make this easy. Surrender, and we will not harm anyone. We only want your freight. Once we transfer as much as we can use, we will release you, and you can be on your way. No damage."

Giving him a smile on the screen that she knew he could see, she put a finger to her head as if thinking. "Well, it seems the word of a marauder is not very strong." She changed the shape of her hand into the gun mode as if shooting herself in the head. She hit the off button, deciding that any conversation with this desperado was useless.

"Deak, only return fire." Giving that order meant that her Weapons Master could not fire first. He would have to wait until the other ship cut loose with a blast before returning a salute. They didn't have to wait long. Their big freighter was a great target, and the shields lit up from two quick blasts. But the hits were on the back wings, as the raider had misjudged the speed of their escaping spaceship.

They also misjudged the fact that the behemoth ship was equipped with more impressive weapons than usual. Deak had done some training inside a virtual unit and now was on his own with all the power of a battle cruiser. He zoomed in on the side of an engine of the privateer and ran a succession of hits.

One blast would have merely flickered their shield, but a group, one after the other and very fast, weakened the protection. Finally, a blast broke through, and there was an eruption. Like all fires in space, it was short as the air was used up in that portion of the ship. Door locks closed down to save the rest of their crew, and the raiders were drifting.

The next thing that happened was another alarm and contact. The alarm was not loud—it was the standard *need for help* sent out by any ship that was stranded.

"We're being hailed, Captain," Mark One said through her head bob again.

"Well, we are going to keep heading to our next jump point, but go ahead and put him through." Kina watched the same face come up, but the gentleman didn't look as calm.

"What the hell are you flying over there, Captain?" His voice sounded a bit hoarse. Perhaps it was from the smoke she saw drifting up to the vents behind him. That meant the inside fire was under control.

"Well, sir, the *Eclipse Shayde* is a full-size freighter carrying supplies and other items on consignment. Of course, we are also equipped to protect our client's items, as we are under contract to deliver all items without damage. I'm sure you understand all about contracts." Kina kept her face in a formal straight expression, not showing any emotion, even though she had a lot of anger inside at the idiot who had blasted at an innocent freighter out in the deep dark.

The man sat back and smiled. "So, are you going to offer the service or tow to an injured spaceship?"

"Unfortunately, Captain." Kina returned his smile. "Being only a freighter, I regret that we will be unable to offer a tow. But we have carefully taken vids of your ship, and my AI has marked your location on the star maps. When we reach civilization, we will send either the Military or Law Enforcement to rescue you immediately."

The man sat back, shook his head, and laughed. "I'm Captain Scott Linares of the ship *One Time*. May I have your name, since you introduced your ship, the *Eclipse*?"

There had to be some stuffing inside a man who was on a stranded ship but could still smile. "I'm Captain Kina Russel. I have to say that I would prefer that we never meet again, but I do wish you well."

"Hmm," Linares nodded. "Yes, I was hoping to treat you to a drink at your next stop. Most of the captains I face out here are not beautiful women that blast my ship out of service. Oh well, maybe in another life. Good trip, Captain."

Hitting the cut button, Kina looked over and found Deak looking at her with a wide grin. He had been released from the weapon enclosure seat and now could sit upright.

The rest of the trip was quiet, and as they'd promised, the crew of the *Eclipse Shayde* reported a stranded spaceship to the control tower. To Kina's raised eyebrows, the man at the other end of the comm who took the information didn't seem interested. He said he would pass the star plot on to the law when his shift was done.

The planet Marheineke was a large world with a slightly lighter gravity. It had small groups of settlements, with each having its own law force and individual governments. The group that had ordered a substantial shipment in hold two of the Eclipse was one of the more prominent places, almost a city. It had a large flat area that would handle the landing for a freighter as big as the *Eclipse*. So, with the AI's help, Kina took their ship slowly through the atmosphere and down to a soft landing.

The planet was getting organized and forming enough law

enforcement to keep the privateers and marauders away. But there was still enough good traffic to and from the area that drew raiders to wait in the deep dark. That was probably why there was not too much enthusiasm from the law going out to tow a stranded ship.

"They probably hope that if it is a raider ship, everyone will die out there in the cold." Deak was adding his comments to Kina's thoughts about the inactivity and interest in a ship that required aid.

"Besides," added Deak. "That captain that took a liking to you has probably called a buddy and is already far away from that location now. I think we'd better hope we don't run into him again."

"Who are we running into?" It was Briget, standing in the opening of the door lock of the bridge. Getting funny looks from the others, she shrugged. "Anyways, I checked, and we have a two-day layover to unload everything from Bay Two. We also will be taking on two small crates. So I want to hit a bar. Let's all go together and see what the locals look like on Marhindend or whatever they call this ass end planet."

Getting out of his seat, Deak was all smiles. "Sounds good. Give me time for a quick shower. Are we hooked up to local power and water?"

"Yep." Briget seemed almost insulted, as if she hadn't done her job correctly. "Use as much water as you need to get rid of your stink."

Looking over at Kina, she winked. "Us ladies also need showers, but only to add perfume. How about it, Cap? Will you be ready in a half hour?"

"Oh." Kina turned in the seat that was now loose. "I hate to leave the ship unoccupied."

"Naw." Briget frowned.

"Sure, Cap. Mark One will handle things and protect the ship. Right, Mark?" Deak's voice was loud as he was making his way toward the exit.

"It would be my pleasure, Captain. I will secure the rest of the ship and cause an electrical field around any area off limits to the ground crew that is unloading and loading. It is standard procedure, whether a crew is on board or not."

Kina looked at the speaker and wondered if the male voice didn't sound a little bit firmer. Could a simply-programmed ship's AI have been developing some bit of emotions?

Feeling that she was boxed in and it would almost be an insult to her crew not to go off-ship with them, she nodded and followed Deak down the hall to her cabin.

An hour later, in civilian clothes, Briget had hailed a local land vehicle for a ride, and they were heading for what the driver said was a good restaurant.

The driver left them off in front of a busy-looking place and took off as soon as they were out of his vehicle. As they looked around, they began to wonder if they were in the wrong part of town.

CHAPTER EIGHT

"Well, as long as we're here, we might as well go inside." Briget led them as a tight group through the door. There were tables with covers of different colors, and most were occupied. A bar was located along one sidewall that was doing a brisk business. Since no one greeted them, Briget, in front, headed through some tables to one that was available.

They had hardly settled down when a waiter came over and set down three big mugs of what looked like beer in front of them.

"You guys need anything else?" He was staring at Kina with a half-smile that was almost an invitation.

"Ah, yeah. The driver who brought us here said that you had some good food." Deak was talking, but the waiter did not take his eyes off Kina.

"Good." The waiter now broke into a full smile. "You will like tonight's fish platter." It was as if he was ignoring the other two and speaking only to Kina. Then he nodded and turned to walk away, grabbing a couple of empty mugs from another area. He didn't bother to clear the entire empty table.

"Well, Cap, you've got an admirer. At least we're going to eat."

Briget had a knowing look on her face. Both she and Deak picked up their mugs and tipped them in a salute to their captain.

To their amazement, the beer was good, and the food was even better. The fish had been fried in a crisp coating, and the local vegetables were butter coated. The special attention that

Kina was getting was beginning to be an embarrassment, but everything was a pleasant evening until a fight broke out.

The three of them had no idea who started the fight or who was involved, but they were affected. A body was slammed across their table, and they were all thrown off their seats, each flying in different directions.

As Deak rose from his broken chair, he was slugged by a man who was throwing fists at anyone the man could reach. Deak took the hit and turned to slam the chair he picked up against the man, who went down. Briget was ducking under the table as feet danced around them, and she saw a knife-wielding guy heading for the door. She knew someone was probably dead.

Crawling out beside Deak, she grabbed him to the side so that he avoided being hit by a bottle that sailed through the air. The whole room was one big brawl. "Deak, we need to get out of here."

"Yea, grab the Cap, and I'll make a path." With that, Deak picked up another chair and turned the legs out in front of him.

As Kina felt everything going backward with the fat guy hitting the middle of her table, she was thrown back, but caught her momentum. Then, in an awkward movement, she leaned forward, let the chair continue away from her, and was on her feet. She lost sight of both of her people, and the noise level was ridiculous. Two more people, a man, and a woman were struggling over something, and she stepped away from them.

Being bumped by a man who was going down, she tried to get a solid footing as she looked around for her crew. In the mess of everyone standing up and a bunch of drunks that wanted to fight, it was hard to see her friends. She thought she saw Deak with a chair in his hands when someone slammed her again. A man who was stepping back to swing a bottle at someone else stepped into her, knocking her sideways, but she gave him a push.

Suddenly he turned and, with a wild yell, swung the bottle at her. With no place to go and no time to duck, a hand reached over her shoulder to hit the wrist, and the bottle and arm flew away in a different direction. The same arm encircled her neck and drew Kina backward against a large body. She was quickly pulled back past all the fighting bodies and through the door to the dark hall that led to the restrooms and back exit.

There was a swift movement, and Kina realized that whoever had hold of her was turning so that he could escape. He was going to let go of her and slip out the back door before she could turn around or catch him. Based only on her instincts, she knew with clarity that this was her stalker.

Oh, if she told anyone else this wanderer had followed her to such an off-the-route place, they would think her crazy. But this shadow had been her nightmare for too long, and she felt he had some unusual way of being at her side wherever she traveled.

What she did next was a surprise and probably stupid. As he lifted her off the ground, she stuck her legs out and caught a foot in the indentation of one of the restroom doors. This stopped the movement, as her foot was jammed, and he needed to pull her back to get her foot loose. But if he went back, he would be up against the closed door to the busy room out front.

With her other foot, she was able to make a big kick up against the doorframe. This caught her assailant by surprise, and they both went down.

"Stop," Kina yelled. "Wait." Twisting, she felt him lie still, and she slowly got up. It was too dark with the doors closed, but she didn't need to see him to know this was her hated shadow.

"Okay, I'm not fighting." Kina held her hands and moved away to give her pursuer room to stand.

He did, in a swift slide that showed her how strong he was, as he used one hand on a sidewall.

"Go ahead and kill me if that is what this is all about." These last words were said in a sad, soft voice as Kina lowered her arms to her side.

Now she waited, and he did reach out to her, taking her by her upper arms. He was tall, probably six foot five or six inches tall, so as a tall woman, she still tilted her head to look up at him. She would not go out with a bow—she was too proud.

What happened next was hard to explain. He almost lifted her off the ground as he shifted her sideways while he also moved down the hallway. At last, she got a glimpse of wide blue eyes that had dark lashes around them. Those eyes had seen a lot and looked down at her with little emotion.

"You are wrong." His voice was quiet, as if he chose not to let anyone but her hear his words. "My job is to protect you."

With these deep words, he released her and moved silently out the back door. Standing there in shock, Kina had to wonder what the hell had just happened.

Finally, shaking herself, she realized she needed to find her friends. But she decided the best route was to also take the back door out. From there, she waited a moment under the light over the building's exit in a quiet alley and saw a way to the front. It was a narrow path between the two buildings that seemed to be empty. Her shadow was gone, so if he was watching her, it was from a distance.

The front of the restaurant was a strange sight. She noticed a lot of people on the outside and more joining them. Most seemed stunned, some needed some first aid, and a few wanted to get away as fast as possible. In the middle of the street were a few people that seemed to be a little less drunk, and among them were Briget and Deak.

"Hey," Kina yelled out as she waved to get their attention.

"Cap, where did you come from?" Deak pushed aside a couple helping each other to walk and rushed over to Kina.

"I was pulled out through the back door. I'll tell you all about it when we get back to the ship." She latched onto both of them as she spoke, and all three began to move away from the fracas. They made their way in what they hoped was the general direction of where the ship was docked.

They passed people trying to get into vehicles, and some were too drunk to operate any. Suddenly, Briget stopped and pulled them over to a floating empty cab that was tilted against a pole where it had stopped.

"Let's try *Grand Auto Theft* and get a ride to the ship." She pulled on the door lock that opened both sides. Looking around, Kina didn't see anyone coming towards them or yelling, so she climbed into the back and let Deak get in next to Briget. Between the two of them, they soon had the cab backing up, turning around, and heading down the middle of the street. They kept the vehicle floating a few feet off the ground and at a moderate speed as they traveled past some lit buildings and lots of dark, closed homes and offices. It took them longer to get back to where the ship was parked than the trip to the restaurant. Eventually, after a lot of backing up and changing directions, they saw the lights of the field where ships were landing.

It was while they were climbing the ramp into the ship that they watched the vehicle pull away. Briget had found a *home* map and sent in the return directions for automatic. They put some loose coin on the front seat and sent it on its way.

"Welcome aboard, team," the voice of Mark One, the ship's AI announced. "We have not completed the new upload in the small bay. I have kept the inside of the ship locked down, and even with your return, I suggest we take precautions with strangers on board."

"Good idea. Keep everything closed and locked behind us and ensure that everyone leaves the ship after all crates are on board. I want a full scan of the new shipment. Confirm that there is nothing alive in any of the crates they brought on board our ship." After her experience in the brawl in the restaurant and the strange comment from her pursuer, Kina was on edge and nervous.

Making their way together through the ship, Deak added a comment. "I don't think any of those drunks we punched back there can even remember our faces, let alone follow us this far away. I think we are fine, Cap."

"It isn't drunks I'm worried about." Kina sighed as she reached the bridge and walked over to the pilot's chair. "It was my stalker who pulled me out of that chaos and hauled me out the back door. That shadow has been able to find me no matter where we go. He has some type of spatial travel machine or something. It is spooky."

Kina shivered as she sat down and turned to look at the others.

"Well, fuck," Deak cursed as he went to his seat. "I guess we need to send in a report to security. Do we also report to the local law?"

With a snort, Briget leaned back against the rear wall. "I hear the law is great on Marheineke if you had coins for a bribe. I think I would keep the report internal and only with our people."

"Damn." Kina slammed her hand on the dashboard hard enough to cause some lights to come on.

"Hey, easy, Cap. Did he try to hurt you?"

Briget leaned forward for her spot on the wall, showing genuine concern.

"You're a beautiful woman. I could see where someone would be out to get to know you in the wrong way. What had our security group reported?"

"That's the problem. No one has been able to find out anything about this ghost. It is why I was transferred to this ship. I was a pilot with a great crew for two years on one of the passenger liners." She gave a big sigh and rubbed her sore hand. "They have never been able to get a facial vid of him on any camera or zoom shot. I was considered a risk to the company because he was able to take the place of a crewman for one jump."

Deak nodded. "Oh, so that's why they put a captain with such a high rating over in the shipping department."

"So, you got away from him at the back of the restaurant?" Briget was still putting together information as she was working on her wrist comm.

"Well, he sort of let me go as I was resisting. I stopped and told him I gave up and for him to go ahead and kill me. He said that his intent was not to harm me but to protect me." Kina was looking down at her hands as she rubbed them together.

"Wait, did he say what he was protecting you from?" Briget asked, but when Kina looked up, both sets of eyes were staring at her intently.

"No. He left, and I came out in the back alley, and I was alone. As usual, he had disappeared. He has got to have some fantastic special equipment that no one else has seen." She raised her head with her eyebrows up. "How else can he stop all those cameras from getting copies of him? How can he disappear so fast, even from our good security people or some of the better local cops? How can he possibly travel along with where I'm going?" Kina's voice was angry.

"Perhaps he's always going with you." Deak now turned and began to bring up some special cameras for the outside of the large freighter. That was where they found a surprise.

Chapter Nine

The large uneven ship had lots of different areas to observe and many cameras that turned around to inspect every inch of the extra-size freighter. What was unusual was that it didn't take Deak long to find some marks on one side that should not be there.

"That son-of-a-bitch has been hooking rides on all of my trips. Where is he now?" Kina looked over at Deak for answers.

"Who knows?" Deak was busy flipping through all the outside cameras, looking for any views that would show damage on their ship or something out of the ordinary.

Briget was busy typing into her wrist comm. "Well, we have to report this to Home Security. We can't have someone attaching or hooking things to the outside of our ships. They could put illegal items on for transport to other destinations."

"They could attach bombs and take us out altogether," added Deak, who was now searching more slowly and taking in-depth looks.

Kina was still concentrating on the guy with the wide chest who had held her in the dark hallway. "What type of vehicle does this asshole have?"

"Whatever he has, it is far beyond normal. To be able to attach to our ship and not get a report from the ship's AI was amazing. And if you tell me that our security and law enforcement had trouble with cameras getting an ID of his face, that means he had tech that had to be equal to or above what our Special Ops people carry. This guy is beyond scary. Are we sure he is from this dimension?" Deak was now doing some serious searching of the outside of the ship.

They all felt the ship tremble as something big was brought into the loading bay. Deak immediately brought up the bay on a big solid overhead screen, and they all looked as a heavy auto hauler set down a crate that didn't look exceptionally large.

"That sucker must weigh a lot. What does the manifest say is in it?" Briget finally quit working her wrist comm as she stepped forward to lean over the others' shoulders to look at what must be a hefty crate. "I'd better go back and make sure that is tied down safely. That shit sliding around could damage one of my engines." With these words, Briget left.

Looking after the engineer, Kina didn't even know if Briget had taken time to send off a report to Home Security.

"Deak, if that is a container that can hold atmosphere, that damn stalker can be inside our ship right now." Kina was staring up at the screen, watching the large hauler back out of the ramp. Briget hadn't had enough time to reach the bay.

But her crewman was fast. He hit his dashboard. "Mark One, ask the hauler to stop. We don't want it to leave yet."

"Confirm." The male voice of the AI responded, and at the same time, some information was flashing inside the loading bay. The big AI of the ship was talking and stopping the limited AI handling the hauler.

"Come on, Cap. Let's go back and help our engineer check out that new load before we accept it." With that, Deak grinned and got up to lead the way through the big ship and off to a side hall to the bay that was open.

After all this time, dawn was finally bringing some pale light across the buildings and through a cloudless sky. The lights around the strange landing zone were still on, but the sky highlighted the few long low buildings and other ships.

By the time Kina and Deak made their way to the side bay

that was open, Briget was looking at the manifest on a pad. She looked up as they came rushing down the metal steps from the inner door lock.

"What does the paperwork say?" Kina yelled out and even got an echo in the large metal room. The use of the word paperwork was an anarchistic leftover from when paper was used as a writing surface. No one would produce the expensive wood product now for such a wasteful purpose that did not last. Everything was kept electronically or on film files. Archives were copied and stored in tiny molecules on drives that could hold more information than an entire civilized world could develop and save. Still, some idioms were spoken to represent a particular use or need.

"Hey, Cap. It says this crate is hermetically sealed and not to be opened except by the receiver on Frica II." The engineer looked up at her captain. "That is a very large station, if you haven't been out that far in the fringe. Still, it is unusual to ship anything heavy to a space station. Going on, it guarantees it is not dangerous or explosive but full of rare metals that are needed beyond the station's site. It doesn't say who will transport it beyond Frica."

The engineer looked at the stalled loader and then at her two friends. "What do you think, Cap?"

"Mark One," Kina called out.

"At your service, Captain." The deep voice answered close to them from a speaker on a loader of their own.

"Can you scan inside this container?" By this time, Kina had approached the crate and was amazed at the solid round corners of a solid metal container. It almost looked to be in one piece.

"Processing, Captain. Please have everyone step back for unusual procedure."

Mark One seemed serious, and all three took several steps back. There were several ways of scanning items inside a bay, all for the safety of the ship. Some of those operations would kill any living thing within the action. This was regular activity on a Shayde freighter and approved by the Federated Military to prevent contamination.

Although the many undertakings of the ship's AI were quick, some were visible blue or green lights passing over the container. It still took several moments before the AI spoke.

"Captain, I was unable to penetrate the interior. I would suggest refusing this shipment per the safety guidelines of Shayde Shipping." The AI then stopped reporting.

The engineer and the Weapons man looked around and then at the captain. Kina nodded. "Okay, we heard our AI. We can't accept this container for shipping. Notify the Shipping Agent and have that big hauler remove the crate. As soon as we have everything clear with the dock, we will leave, since we do have other items to deliver and a schedule to keep."

Stopping in the galley to fill a mug with coffee, she got a ping on her wrist comm. It was from Briget so she waited until she got to the bridge to call the engineer back.

"Captain, we have a problem—no we have *problems*."

Bringing up the permanent screen that Deak had set up to view the side bay, she saw both of them still there with the container and the big hauler. Nothing had moved or changed except for Deak who was pacing back and forth.

"Report," Kina demanded, using the ship's speakers.

Briget held up the pad with the manifest and all the shipping information. "The agent says that the shipper is no longer available. Seems that the mysterious shipper has become incommunicado and has no forwarding information. All contact will be at the other end when the package is delivered."

"Okay, get that big hauler back up and running, and we will leave the carton sitting out in the sunshine," Kina stated in a calm voice that she didn't feel as she watched Deak walk over and slam a fist on the big inactive hauler.

"No luck, Cap. This beast is dead. We would need a bigger one to move it out of the way to get the carton off the ship." To prove his point as he spoke, he also kicked the side of the useless piece of machinery.

Over the speaker, Kina tried to keep her frustration from showing. "Can we contact the moving company for another hauler?"

"Already talked to them. They say this was their best big guy, and they are accusing us of damage. They say we must remove the hauler from our ship." Briget was waving the pad in the air like she was going to throw it at the hauler.

"Captain, I have Home Security on a direct line for you." It was the serene deep voice of Mark One.

"Good, put them up on my direct screen." Kina waited as the permanent screen in front of her chair lit up and the face of a man in the uniform of a security lieutenant appeared.

"I understand you have a problem, Captain."

"Well…" Kina hesitated and then decided on the whole truth. "If you are aware of my file, I have a stalker. He has shown up on this docking site but escaped as usual without a trace. My Weapons Officer has found traces on the outside of our ship that some type of unit has been attached. Nothing is there at this time, and we have all outside cameras on full guard." She stopped to see if the man was following her.

The man asked the obvious question. "Have your people checked around your location?"

"With a lot of activity around us, we have not noticed anything that would match a small survival component. After that, we received a small but very heavy sealed container for shipment. It is so unusual and brings a lot of questions, including the safety of the ship. It could contain a survival system inside. It is extremely heavy and can't be moved except by a large hauler. The hauler that delivered it has died on our open ramp, and the moving company claims there is nothing available big enough to remove the hauler. They claim we are responsible since they claim we might have done something to the hauler. This falls under the guidelines of the shipping manual of not accepting dangerous items. I am sending you a view of the bay with the container and the hauler."

The lieutenant studied the file and then muted the mic as he talked to someone else in his room. At last, he came back to speak to Kina.

"Captain Russel, how good a pilot are you? By that question, I don't want the answer you give quietly to a Board of Inquiry. I want the one you give to the guys when you are all out after several beers and swapping tales."

Hesitating only a moment, Kina decided he wanted a truthful answer. "I'm the best, Lieutenant."

"Good. Here is what you are going to do to protect the freighter *Eclipse Shayde* and its crew."

Mark One and Captain Russel listened to the lieutenant's instructions and followed them to the letter. First, Captain Russel made sure her crew was in safe positions. The engineer was closed up in a special holding area near Briget's favorite control panel, enclosed by safety harnesses.

Deak had hurried up through the ship to join the captain on the bridge and was now almost unseen in his seat. The pilot's chair had adjusted to allow Kina to run the ship in a mode that would keep her safe in the next few unusual moves.

"Mark One, lock up the ship as instructed."

"Confirm and done, Captain." The loud sound of double door locks closing and locking as the AI of the ship did what the captain and the security lieutenant had decided was necessary. The small bay of the ship was going to be left open, but it was going to be left double-sealed off from the rest of the ship until the package within it had been delivered.

First, Kina contacted control at the docking zone and, without permission, informed them of the departure of *Eclipse Shayde*. Next, she took the ship off slowly in a normal glide over the other ships and low buildings. Once clear of buildings and activity, Kina did the unusual and rare maneuver.

Using the strong-steering engines, she turned the nose straight up and blasted away. This was in the manner of ancient rockets, taking straight off from worlds before the control of gravity.

At about eight thousand feet, there was the shift, as a heavy hauler slid off and out the open back. The strange dark carton was still in place on the floor of the bay. Well, they would leave the bay open to the void and cold of space until they landed on the space station that wanted something ponderous.

The engineer could get up through the ship by using a side crawl opening along the walls of the ship. This allowed Briget to get to the galley and the bridge and join the others for company. She did express pride in how well the ship performed on the unusual exit from a world, and still, every engine was in top shape. They all looked at the cameras on the small bay where the carton sat as if an evil threat. All they had to do was survive a couple of jumps and get to a small space station.

Chapter Ten

The docking and unloading at the station were almost a disappointment. The carton was taken out the back in weightless space with a hauler, put into another smaller ship, and was gone. The correct paperwork was handled, and payment was complete. If the captain's stalker had been in that carton, he never got out into the ship, and the crew decided not to leave the ship.

They locked up everything tight, did a complete search of the outside of the ship, and left for their next delivery. There was an acknowledgment from Mark One that they were clear and ready for their first jump.

With Briget back in engineering, Deak sitting in the next chair, Kina gave the notice and hit all the right buttons. She sat back and looked at the black and white pictures of the outside of the big freighter. Out in deep space, there was only the light that was attached to each camera to show a strange path across the ship, which was either black or dark metal.

"I will say you have added some excitement to our old tub since becoming our captain." Deak was also looking at the outside screens. "The only thing we used to do was shoot back at a stupid pirate."

"So, you did run into pirates out here?" Kina reached for her coffee mug without taking her eyes off the screen. For the next couple of hours, as they approached the jump point, they swapped stories. Taking the last sip of cold coffee, she froze her screen and got up.

"I'm going to the ladies' room and then get some coffee to

fill my bladder again. You want more when I come back?" Kina had taken a couple of steps when Deak's words stopped her.

"What's that?"

Turning, she looked at his screen and saw, in the sharp black and white shadows, a perfectly rectangular box on the metal of their ship.

"Mark One, confirm the identity of highlighted item," Deak said calmly, but she felt his tension.

"Unknown, Crewman Warvel."

To hell with coffee. Kina stepped back, setting the mug on the dashboard. "Mark One, can you give us information on that item? What is its size?"

"Captain, it is what you would call a small item. A box about two inches or five point zero eight centimeters by six inches or fifteen point two four centimeters by three inches or seven point six two centimeters. That is a rectangular metal box attached firmly to that particular position of the ship." Mark One rattled off the dimensions without hesitation.

Deak looked over at Kina and shook his head. "Like I said, excitement."

Frowning at her crewman, Kina had an idea. "Mark One, can one of your drones or automatons go out and retrieve that item?"

"I can send several different types of drones out to get close scans of the item to see if it can be penetrated with different wavelengths. But since it seems to be attached strongly enough to ride through the jumps and different systems, I don't believe it can be extracted. But we might find some way to open it. But if there are explosives involved, that could be dangerous, so I must warn you of damage and possible atmosphere leak."

"Damn." With that information, Kina sat back down in her chair. She needed some hot coffee.

"Too much excitement," Deak muttered.

"Okay, we can at least get some scans and maybe some information. Mark One, get out some drones to look at that box. I want whatever you have that might penetrate different types of metal. Also, get a sniffer out there to see if there is any trace of standard explosives. I'm going to bring us to a full stop."

"Conform, Captain." Mark One probably already had drones in the air, as it was so reactive.

Kina used her wrist comm to bring Briget up to date, and the ship was soon dead in space, though that was not a true statement. It still drifted, but there was nothing close to make a comparison for the ship's movement.

In a side workroom near the back of the ship where Briget had set up some equipment, they spent hours analyzing the information that the drones sent back to the AI.

"So, there are no traces of the standard explosives. But it does hum." Deak was looking at all the films with the different traces on them. They were useless.

"The hum is extremely faint. I don't think the human ear would hear it." Briget was looking at the symbols of the noise.

"Right, okay. Does anyone have any idea? I'm not going to send any of us out there to touch it." Kina leaned a hip against another tall table. She looked at Deak.

"Well, Cap, if it is a bomb, it is a small one, so I think it is meant to blow a small hole in that spot, and it will slow us down for pirates or someone else. I vote for a small bomb with the timer electrical and counting down as a hum." Deak ended his theory with a nod.

"But that isn't even in a weak place." Briget snorted. "It might make a hole and not even slow us down. I think it is full of poison and it will be slowly let loose through the metal of the ship. I think the hum is acid, eating into the metal to release the poison inside."

"It's too small." Kina frowned but was grateful that they had a good coffee maker down here. She sipped her coffee for a moment. "If it had acid to eat into the ship, that would fill up the little box. No, it's something else." She looked up at the speaker overhead.

"Do you have a theory, Mark One?"

"I do, Captain. I am honored that you asked for my conclusion. It is a simple tracker."

The three humans looked at each other and then up at the speaker. Of course, the AI was correct. Something small and easy to attach to the ship. A small box with a hum that was just the inside wavelengths that humans couldn't hear, sometimes the simple answer was the correct one.

"Hey, Cap. I think I need some firing practice." Deak walked out of the room and headed for his cabin.

The next time Kina saw him, he was in an off-ship suit and was clomping around on the outside of the ship with a long gun. Every so often, he would let go of a shot as if aiming for a distant star or asteroid. At last, on one screen, she saw the results of his hit against the edge of their ship.

After a couple of tries, the heavy weapon blasted the small box away from the metal of the *Eclipse*. There was a rough misshaped place on the outside of the ship that would eventually have to be addressed once they docked, but there was no internal damage.

During the routine segments of the rest of their flight, Deak spent his time carefully searching the outside of the ship. Mark One also did some internal searches, and both reported nothing. But all four felt uneasy. For an AI to have doubts was a first. They completed the next jump and were heading through normal space for another jump with one more distraction.

"Captain, we have company," Mark One announced in Kina's cabin.

She had just come out of a shower and was getting into her clean suit.

"Okay, thanks. I'll be on the bridge momentarily. Request for Crewman Warvel to come to the bridge also, Mark." She had found it easier to shorten the AI's name.

"Acknowledge, Captain."

By the time both Deak and Kina were down in their seats, Mark One had a couple of solid screens up. They showed the outside, and something so small in the deep dark, it was almost indistinguishable at this time.

"Report, Mark," Kina stated as the seat adjusted around her.

"The ship was inside the system and began to put on a burst of speed. Its trajectory is now directly following our trail. My estimation puts them equal to us within two hours. They are a lighter, faster ship in normal space."

The report was given in a calm male voice. Kina wasn't sure if it helped that the AI didn't sound fake or metallic. Sometimes that calm male voice was irritating.

"Cap." Deak was getting up from the seat she was used to seeing him occupy in dangerous situations. "We have a second Weapons Control Sector on the *Eclipse*. I'm going there now for safety's sake." He picked up a small comm unit from a drawer that Mark One popped open and put it in his ear. "Mark will keep us in close contact."

A small drawer had popped open in front of Kina and held a similar device, so she took it and did the same thing with it, believing in the AI and its help.

Deciding to test it, Kina said, "Briget, are you in contact also?"

"Yes, ready, and I am watching for all power."

Briget almost sounded happy. This was a strange crew. One went into space and cheerfully fired a long gun, and an engineer didn't mind overtaxing her power sources.

As with most problems out in the deep space, everything took a lot of time. Kina drank her coffee, filled in some electronic forms, and watched the dot on one screen grow to a larger dot.

"Damn, I need a fresh cup of hot coffee," Kina muttered out loud as she set the empty mug away from her on the dashboard. She would have jumped if the enclosing seat would have space to allow any movement. A large metal arm reached forward, and it held a tray that had a steaming mug.

"Captain, your coffee." Mark One's voice came from a small speaker in front of the pilot's seat.

"Mark." Kina sighed as she took the mug and smelled the fresh odor. "I think I will have to marry you."

Mark One's voice changed a bit lower. "Thank you, Captain, but I think there might be regulations against such an agreement."

Kina smiled and took a sip of the hot, satisfying drink.

"Captain, we are being hailed," Mark One announced.

Sitting her mug down, Kina straightened up. "Is it our friends from behind us?"

"Acknowledged, Captain."

"Okay, put it through to the small permanent screen on the left of me." Kina looked over at the screen that was on the dashboard. There was some static, but the picture was clear enough to show the face of a man and a chair back. Everything else was fuzzy.

"Freighter. Come to a dead stop. We aren't interested in people or getting rid of any of our expensive ammo, so make this easy. We will board and examine your containers and take a few interesting items. You will be able to go on, and your company's insurance will get a bill. A clean stop with no questions asked. A big guy like you should have a few things you won't mind losing, perhaps a couple of items even your crew could latch onto and keep on the side. Everything out in the deep dark is a secret. So, what do you say? An easy stop?"

Having the long announcement piped over the ship so her two friends could hear everything, Kina had let him talk.

"This is Captain Russel of the freighter *Eclipse Shayde.* I would love to acquiesce to your demands, but there is a serious problem. Unfortunately, you have tried to purloin one of the few ships full of a crew of honest people and a loyal AI. So beware of what you ask for, because surprises can hurt. Out."

Kina smiled at her choice of big words, hoping the scraggly-looking man on the other ship could understand what she had said. Perhaps he had a dictionary on a small pad.

"Deak, I have the small weapons on both sides. You have whatever the big surprises are that you think might be available. I hope it is as good as you promised, because our friend behind us has called up a buddy."

With that, Mark One showed another ship that had been in silent mode and now was in the chase. Damn.

Chapter Eleven

Battles in space were sudden deadly bursts of cannon and then long waits, as ships had to take time to move, turn around and line up to fire again. Unfortunately, space battles were more dangerous than land battles. One piece of debris penetrating a ship that would leave a hole too big to shut out a section would kill everyone on board. The atmosphere would instantly escape faster than the reserve tanks could replace it. A flash fire could consume everything until there was no air to feed the flames.

After they flew at top speed through normal space, the first threat of a burst of a canon flew past the large freighter. The *Eclipse* was too big to miss, but the pirates didn't want to destroy the ship. They wanted it whole and complete to protect the cartons in its big holds.

The marauders made mistakes. They didn't stay together and make their attacks as a solid team. They also didn't expect a large standard freighter to have more than the usual weapons. When the raiders moved in close, Deak, in his special station on what could be called the top of the ship, fired off two shock waves from the ion canon.

The first wave took out the shield of the ship Deak had aimed at and the second wave took out all its power. The ship turned dark even as it continued to move in its original direction. Nothing was going to stop it or change it as the marauder's ship moved through space without power. The entire crew would die if they were not able to get something back up online soon to keep the atmosphere moving.

Apparently it took a few minutes for the second ship to realize that its companion was out of the battle, but finally it moved to the assistance of the dark ship.

"Captain, we have a contact incoming." Mark One had her favorite small screen lit up.

"Go ahead and accept it, Mark." Kina was still getting over the shock of the power of the weapon on her ship. It was the type that was put on important military vessels.

"Captain of the freighter. Be warned." The face of the man on the screen was what one would expect. He needed a shave and was older with a lot of wrinkles, grey in the beard, and long scraggly hair. He had not taken care of himself nor taken any youth treatments.

Looking at one of the tracking screens, she could see that the *Eclipse* was heading in a different direction than the other ships. Mark One had already changed their direction. The dark ship was still going in the straight original route, and the one that was now contacting them had sharply turned off into the distance.

"Be warned. We have you marked, and we will have a bigger group the next time. You will have no contact until you feel our weapons. Beware." With that, he cut the contact, and she was left with a screen full of static.

"Well damn. He isn't very nice." Kina sat back with a smile.

Mark One was now in his normal male voice. "I have recorded everything to forward to our security and Federated Law. Perhaps we should avoid this particular area in the future, Captain."

"We go where the shipments are needed, Mark. Now get us to that jump point. We don't want to be late for our next delivery."

"Captain."

Mark One now spoke in a different voice she had never heard. It was quiet and still male, but younger. "Thank you for accepting an AI as one of your crew."

Sitting and thinking, Kina decided it was because she had started calling the AI by only one name. *Mark.* It must have taken that as a term of closer recognition. She had begun to see that the AI in this ship was more reactive and better able to help with handling the ship than any that she had worked with before.

Fortunately for the nerves of the crew and the sake of the freighter, the rest of the trip to their next delivery point was without any more incidents. But life was not meant to be serendipitous out on the fringe.

When Captain Russel made contact for docking access on the next planet, there was no reply. They did notice a couple of other ships orbiting the planet. One looked like a freighter, and the other was smaller. Mark One brought up on screens some views of small shuttles moving around above the heavy cloud cover that shrouded the planet.

Without communication, there was no way they were going to take their ship down, actually blind, to try to land and unload. Kina and Mark were using every device they had on board and all the frequencies available. Finally, in frustration, Kina had Mark set up an automatic signal and went to the restroom and then the galley.

Briget had joined them and they had settled down to a hot meal when Mark One interrupted them.

"Captain. We have contact from another ship in the nearby vicinity."

"I'll take it on the bridge. Thank you, Mark." Kina got up and dumped her half-eaten plate into the clean-up unit. It was a good plan that the galley was close to the bridge on their immense ship. It took her only a few quick steps to make it up the hallway and through the door lock to reach the bridge. She quickly slipped into her seat and knew that the AI would know she was present.

Her favorite screen lit up and showed a middle-aged clean-cut man who was waiting.

"Sorry, Sir. I was off the bridge. This is Captain Russel of the freighter *Eclipse Shayde.* You made contact?" Kina waited as she felt the seat adjust.

"Hello, Captain Russel. This is Captain Barkowski of the cruiser *Far Crossing Linares.* If this is your first stop at planet Trigo Five, I have assumed you have not received any communication from Landing Control. If not, it is because there is none. This is a very wide place with a lot of lack of discipline. Over?"

"Captain Barkowski, welcome. This is Captain Russel, and yes, it seems to be our first delivery here and in this sector. No special instructions were included. We would appreciate any local information you might be able to share. Over?"

With the advice from a captain who had been in the area over Trigo Five for some time, the crew of the freighter had a good idea of what to expect when delivering items to a customer on this strange planet.

First, Briget and Deak had to take a shuttle down through the clouds to do a search across the planet for any radio announcements for businesses receiving shipments. There were many scrambled announcements, with the radio stations bouncing back below the clouds. The pair made copies of everything, and after a quick spin around near the planet, with a couple of near misses because of a lot of traffic, they returned to the ship.

With the help of AI, they spent a few tedious hours pulling the communications apart.

At last they had a couple of clear broadcasts that were companies that required deliveries that matched what was in cartons in one of their holds.

Kina took the shuttle, downloaded with cartons and an autoloader that had direct control by Mark One. That way, the captain had an extra crew with her on this trip. The shuttle was hard to handle with the excess weight, but there was no need for speed. She was heading to warehouse areas that avoided tall buildings, moving in streams of traffic that seemed to have some unwritten rules. Everything seemed to move along without accidents.

On a corner in broad daylight, shooting began between people in two different land vessels. Kina had no idea what it was all about, and like all the other vehicles in the vicinity, she tried to move as fast as possible away from the turmoil. The effect of the shooting caused someone to overreact, and ahead of her shuttle, two units crashed. There was a tie-up in the area between tall buildings, and everything was jamming up behind, some other vehicles bumping into each other to try to get out of the way.

"Up or down?" Kina was thinking out loud.

Mark spoke to her from the hauler in the back of the bay.

"Down. Everyone else will try to rise, and there will be more problems."

"Good idea." Nodding, Kina changed the motion indicator that acted immediately, and she was soon sliding along the roadbed on treads. Sparks and different types of shadows were above them as they were able to slip under the tangle of transports that was getting worse, as anti-gravity units kept everyone at a preset level.

Being on a level almost by themselves except for pedestrians, Kina kept the shuttle moving slowly until they were far away from the chaos of the shooting episode. After all of this trouble, when she got close to the warehouse that wanted to accept deliveries, there was another problem.

After a lot of strange communications, while Kina sat in the shuttle hidden in an alley several buildings away, they didn't have the correct paperwork. They still insisted they would pay any amount needed and would gratefully accept the delivery.

"Captain, I believe we should leave this area. Some activity seems to be coming in our direction."

"Damn," muttered Kina as she took the heavy shuttle straight up until they were above the warehouse buildings. She quickly had them in a stream of other traffic, moving away from the unfriendly company that wanted her load.

"Well, that was interesting. This is a really strange place, Mark. Let's hope the next company is real and has our funds and the right paperwork. I hate to take a load back home." Kina was driving carefully among so many land vehicles. Even though this world was locked in by deep heavy clouds, it was a dark but busy place. People had thrived in unusual ways, and companies needed deliveries, but some were desperate.

It was another hour before Kina found another sector of warehouses. This area was also where the broadcasts had indicated that a buyer was waiting for a delivery. Again, she found an alley to settle in before contacting the company that had sent out the notices.

The conversation started exactly like the previous one, but this time the company sent a preview of some paperwork.

"Mark, you get to unload those crates." Kina took the shuttle out of their hiding place and went over several buildings to an open warehouse door to land and open the back ramp. While Mark unloaded crates, Kina checked the paperwork and waited for the second half of the payment to be sent.

Since the planet was locked in by the cloud cover, Kina had to take payment on her pad, and she spoke aloud to Mark.

"I see some info. I wonder if my assistant can confirm?"

"Transfer is confirmed and correct." Mark's deep voice was now different, a simple metal from the hauler. The three workers and the man representing the company receiving the load looked at the hauler and Kina, but in their world, they must have seen a lot of strange things. As long as they got their shipment, they were satisfied.

Deciding to get off of this planet as fast as possible, and now in a light shuttle, Kina used full power to take a slight circular flight upward to reach above the atmosphere as soon as she could in a safe manner.

"Captain, we have traffic."

It was Mark, in the metal voice behind her coming from the hauler speaker. It had contact through either the shuttle or maybe the *Eclipse* above. She didn't have time to ask, as before she got any words out, a ship was up beside her. She pulled away, but not only did the small ship move with her, it turned so quickly it bumped against the tail fin of the shuttle.

Fighting for control of her ship, Kina gave instructions to Mark. "Mark, contact the ship for help."

"Acknowledged, Captain." The metal voice was closer as the hauler slid up through the ship to stand behind the front of the cabin.

Chapter Twelve

"Captain, the *Eclipse* is moving, but they are far away. We need to take care." Mark gave Kina the bad news. With a larger ship moving up behind them, and the *Eclipse* still too far away to be of help, Kina had to do some fast action. The shuttle was able to react fast, and that was about its only ability. It did not have weapons, as it was used only for transport.

With a bigger ship on her tail, she had to assume it would also be space worthy. They were still in the stratosphere, skimming above the heavy cloud layer that locked in the planet. Her only choice was to duck back down into the clouds and hope the interference of the water vapor would give her some chance to escape.

If the ship on their ass end had any special equipment, the clouds wouldn't help. But Kina had no choice but to delay until her big ship could come and catch her or knock out her threat. Flying a light ship in heavy cloud cover was not a fun game. The battering of winds and changes of direction from the storms wanted to throw the shuttle out of control, so Kina took manual control.

"Mark, have you received any contact from the ship following us?" Kina was hoping that the bigger ship would avoid the clouds.

"Captain, I get a flicker of the ship in between storm flashes. My best estimate is that it is still following us. I have no contact outside this heavy barrier to reach the *Eclipse*, but they have better apparatus and can penetrate the storms. They will find us as soon as they reach this area." The hauler container with some of the essence of the AI had locked itself right behind Kina's seat.

There was a vicinity notice put up on one screen, and Kina knew it wasn't a warning about the storms around her. The damn larger ship was faster and probably could handle the storms better than her light shuttle. It was closing in on her. Would someone shoot them down on this stupid dark planet?

They had already had some damage on the shuttle, and fighting in these storm clouds meant that the small ship would require more work once it was back in its bay. That was if they ever returned to the home bay. At that point, there was a flash of light that was different from the lightning around them. It was the blast of a canon streaking past them.

Dropping her ship down and pouring all the speed she could apply, she tried to twist from side to side. The storm helped, so she went with the winds and let them throw her away. She hoped that would make the ship a hard-moving target.

"Captain, I am receiving an odd second blip. It also is intermittent, but I am sorry to say it is also very close."

At least Mark One kept the metal voice very soft with its bad news. But bad news continued, as another streak from a canon shot flashed past on their bay side, and Kina turned into that side, hoping to outthink her attackers.

Then in a lull in one of the storms, Kina lifted her little ship up to avoid another blast, and at the same time, her ship was hit by the wave of an explosion behind her.

"What the hell was that?" Kina could not check on any of the dashboard readouts as she was too busy bringing the little ship back on an even keel.

"Captain. The larger ship is no longer with us. I estimate that it was destroyed through some explosion that caused the shock wave that affected us." Mark One did have the time to check both the ship's instruments and some of its own. "But the second ship is now approaching. It seems to be very fast and strong and not affected by the atmosphere."

At last, having the shuttle under some control with small bounces, Kina had to wonder if the second ship had blown the larger one out of existence. If so, she was probably next. But to her surprise, in the stormy dark area of rain and lightning, a strange black shape pulled up beside her. It seemed to match her ship's erratic movements for a moment and then slowly slipped on ahead to disappear into the storms.

"Did you record that, Mark?"

"Acknowledged, Captain."

What they had seen would be hard to describe, a black bullet with very small fins and no portholes or windows. But it seemed to have not meant her shuttle harm and had destroyed a bigger ship that was blasting away in the middle of the planet's heavy clouds.

"No!" Kina yelled, and she pulled the shuttle straight up to escape the gravity well.

"Captain, is there another problem?" The hauler was still clamped on behind her seat.

"That bullet could attach itself to the outside of our freighter." At last Kina slowed the trajectory of the shuttle.

Outside the cover of the planet, her transmission suddenly burst to life. "Shuttle one, this is *Eclipse,* please respond. Shuttle one, we have you on screens so please respond."

Hitting the comm, Kina brought up the connection. "*Eclipse,* this is Shuttle one. It is good to hear your voice, Deak. Come and open the bay door. We have power and will enter under our power."

She decided she would wait until she was back in the safety of the freighter before she discussed the black bullet ship with her team. Landing inside the freighter and watching the hauler roll off and shut down was like coming home. One of the first things Kina was going to do was send in a negative report to the home office and home security. Her recommendation was going to be negative on any shipments to planet Trigo Five. The extra cost of finding the correct receiver did not figure into the delivery price.

After she made those two reports, she needed to have a long talk. She and Mark would have some information to share about her stalker and a black bullet ship. Fortunately, Mark had vids.

"Do you have a navigation site for me to insert, Captain?" Mark One was now speaking through one of the interior ship speakers as she exited the shuttle and started the long trek forward.

"Yes, as soon as everyone is ready, get us on to our next delivery. I need to check our progress and the rest of the routes. I have the plan to put in place." Kina couldn't keep the anger out of her voce—anger at the situation, not at her crew.

For the benefit of everyone, the next circle of the delivery journey took the freighter on a circle that was the last in the dangerous fringe. They had one more on a quiet science space station, and then two more on inner planets that were on the way home.

The deliveries went fairly smoothly, one was paid in full, and the other would not transfer funds until they checked inside the containers, which meant a slight delay. Since everything was approved, they were again on their way and gratefully did not run into any pirates or mercenaries between jumps.

The stop at the outpost of a science station was in an isolated place that allowed the ship to pull up and dock against the hub of the unit. It was an old-fashioned unit with a large rotating wheel for human use that provided gravity, even though the hub had a gravity unit installed. Some programs and tests were being done in the void and without gravity for experiments.

The interesting part was that the large hub had a lot of entertainment, such as bars and restaurants. A lot of military and transport ships stopped by because it was the only place out in this lonely area. Someone had found a way to earn funds.

Telling her crew that she was still recovering from the shuttle episode, she encouraged them to take advantage of the R&R but said she would relax on the ship. A short time after the ship was quiet, Kina went to the small door lock that was on the outside, facing space. The *Eclipse* was docked in at an angle with the nose in tight and a long, enclosed attachment coming from the docking area out. It connected to the side of the bay and made unloading easy.

This position left one whole side of the big freighter and the long top open to space. The ship had many double-safe door locks. Perhaps they had been put in for safety or been installed as the additions had been added with more bays and sections. Coming from her cabin, dressed in a personal comfortable off-ship suit, Kina headed to a small side door lock and entered.

Closing the entry door, she pushed the ready button to start the air withdrawal and allowed her suit to close up over her head and lock into place.

"Captain, is there a problem that you are going outside to investigate?" Mark One asked inside her helmet.

At this point, Kina chose to ignore the AI. When the green light came on, she opened the outside door to the blackness of space. She cut the gravity in the floor and hung onto the handles, working her way to the outside. At the last handle, Kina placed her feet against the wall of the ship and took a deep breath, and then pushed off as hard as she could.

As she expected, momentum in space meant that there was nothing to impede or change a body's trajectory. That meant Kina was traveling away from the *Eclipse* and the station at a steady speed.

"Captain, there must be a problem. You do not have any extra oxygen with you, and I cannot detect any steering containers. Do you require assistance?"

The AI's voice was loud in Kina's helmet. Working her arms up so she could see them through the clear helmet, she hit a couple of buttons on the comm attached.

"Captain, do you—"

With that, she hit the right button to cut off the contact with the AI. She didn't need to hear Mark as he called out to her. She knew she was making a problem for the AI, but he would handle it. She could imagine him working within the ship, sending out signals trying to reach her in different manners and levels.

Calming herself down, expecting to have a long wait, Kina did not expect to have anything happen until she was really in deep trouble. That meant she had to float away from the station for a couple of hours before her air began to get low. Settling down to study distant stars and thinking about her previous jobs got boring, and when she checked her comm, only about forty-five minutes had passed.

Now she began to sing songs to herself. Kina smiled and sang loudly, hoping that would use up more air. If her stalker was monitoring her, surely he would know when she was in the danger zone. But time was relative, and eventually, she did begin to get the warning signal up on her helmet screen.

Her question was, how long would he wait to pick her up? Worse, what if she was wrong and he wasn't in the area? She was going to die out here to prove a wrong point. Her air began to taste funny. Things began to look darker even than the deep dark space.

Chapter Thirteen

When she opened her eyes, she was on her stomach, and someone was removing her helmet the hard way, trying to tear it off.

"Hey, press the button," Kina muttered as she tried to free her hands. Someone was holding her down, and they were inside a ship. The body holding her down was gone, and she finally hit a release to get her helmet off. Fresh air rushed in, and she gulped a large breath.

With her body getting strong and her head clear with the air, Kina rolled over with the help of someone's hands. To her shock, it was in the hands of a Shayde Security guard. Standing behind the female guard, who also had her helmet off, were several other guards, some in off-ship suits.

"Where are we?" she asked as she got up and looked around at the hallway inside a ship. They were near what was probably the side door lock unit.

"Where, uh, are we alone?" Kina stumbled over her words. This was not quite what she had expected. She was sure that when she went out into the deep space with limited air, her stalker would do his thing. He would save her at the last minute, and she hoped he would take her on his special ship.

"Captain Russel, using yourself as bait may not be safe or smart, but it did work. We have your stalker in a special cell. Good going." The security guard had a stripe on her off-ship suit that told Kina that the woman was a sergeant. That meant the sergeant was probably in charge of this group.

They led Kina back through what she soon recognized as a

military ship to the med area. She was left to get out of the suit and be examined by a live doctor. Several hours later, and in a new Shayde uniform, a lower-grade young man had escorted her to the standard military mess area. Kina had to admit she was taken aback to find Shayde had an entire military unit.

Everyone had on uniforms of the guard division that served wherever the top officials at Shayde felt their security was needed. Such a big corporation with headquarters on several planets had found that the local law officials weren't up to handling inter-system problems.

As Kina was finishing up a delicious meal, the sergeant that had helped her at the door lock where they'd pulled her aboard approached.

"Captain Russel." The woman acknowledged her and stood. "The report from med says you are in good shape. That is good news. We are going to transport the prisoner on a small, fast ship back to a special location. They would like you to go along so you can file some final reports and give some DNA tests."

Nodding in agreement, Kina rose and followed the sergeant and several others. DNA tests were not only a look at the lattice to see who you were. There was also history buried in the blood and stories to be read. With modern equipment and trained people, there was so much to learn from a smear of blood.

They made their way down through the narrow busy halls to the bays, choosing a side that held small jump ships. One ship had a crew working around it as she was led over to the back side entrance. Two guards entered and sat down in the small area across from each other. They were in full combat armor, with weapons available. There was a small amount of shifting as they got the weapons into position, and then they sat up stiffly.

She entered and took the other seat that was across from him. The prisoner was not restrained, because he was in a seat behind a shimmering but transparent wall. It was a deadly gamma bubble. It was simply a killer. Touch it from the inside, and you would be knocked unconscious. Try to break out of it, and you would be hit so hard with electricity you would have to be resuscitated by a med. If the right person didn't move or change it, it would implode and kill anything inside. It was a perfect restraint.

As she sat, she glanced at him, seeing him fully for the first time. His right brow was a bit arched, and his lips were grim but full. One of the things her eyes caught was his calloused and scarred hands.

This told her he was used to physical exertion. Something was wrong with this male. His hair was long and pulled back to a loose knot at his neck.

Kina glanced away for a breath as her body reacted in strange ways that she recognized. Adrenaline was released as if she was in danger or for some other reason she didn't understand. She shook her shoulders as a chill ran across her face.

She saw a slow movement as he slowly turned until he stared at her. Something feral, as well as unsavory, now surfaced through the depths of his glimmering eyes. Worse, there was humor sparkling alongside a violent light. He was a ferocious powerhouse in incredibly confined quarters.

As if he were reading her mind, his lips pulled into a smile with perfectly straight white teeth. His head turned back slowly until he was looking out the window again, still smiling but now at nothing.

A shiver of fear dumped more adrenaline into her body. How long was their ride in this small, fragile jump ship?

As if the man had heard her thoughts, his lips pulled into a wider smile. Kina shifted nervously in her seat. The guards seemed to perk up to attention, watching both of them closely. They obviously recognized that something was wrong. Hard not to miss the signals. The lunatic was sitting right there, smiling at nothing.

A burst of perspiration erupted along her brow. At least the uniform took care of her heat. "We need to adjust the heat in here," Kina stated out loud. The prisoner started to chuckle, of all things.

"We are five minutes out, Captain," the left guard said, eyes wide as they both shifted weapons in front of them.

"I didn't ask for ETA. I need the heat adjusted."

"Yes, of course, Captain. I apologize." The left guard turned and palmed the screen next to the partition. He entered a code and then sat up straight again.

Kina assumed that he had done something with the cooling system. Perhaps it was off due to the restraining bubble.

She nodded to show she'd taken the info. Kina would try to stay unaffected until the worst case.

What is the worst case?

Kina eyed the smiling madman. His head sat higher than the guards, indicating he was taller and had a longer reach. With that breadth of shoulder and those arms stacked with muscle, his movements would be powerful. Fast? Probably. She had to assume the worst. A launch from those thick legs, and he'd be on her lap before she knew it.

That was assuming the tech didn't work. But he had done some strange things with tech in the past. She tried to be ready, remembering all of her training. Even a man as big as the one sitting so close to her should be paralyzed by bubble technology. Regardless, it would take him time, if he tried, to break through the invisible barrier, and in that time, she had her hand on a knife. It was the only weapon they had let her keep. In that small window of time, she could stab him.

Her pulse throbbing, she took a deep breath and prepared for the worst. The soft shudder of the vessel docking startled her.

The guards removed Kina first, and she was put in a vehicle and taken across the flat-covered landing zone. Although the system was different, Kina felt at home. The guards took her to the standard hotel for personnel of Shayde. They were located on one of the planets that was on the edge of the center group. That meant it was busy, important, and overcrowded. This was Glover II and had two moons, one that was also settled.

With such a large population, the law was strong, and the military had a significant presence. The Shayde Corporation was not the only large company with a foot in the hectic and prosperous world. On the streets, it was common to see as many people in some type of uniform as individuals in civilian clothes.

Criminals who were so desperate or stupid as to commit an offense in this area were often surrounded by different enforcement groups. Action in the courts on Glover II was quick and efficient, as any prosecution charged against the perpetrator was complete with proof. Modern equipment supported by intelligent forensics.

Becoming part of the proof system, Kina again found herself in a medical facility.

For the next eight days, between meals and sleeping periods, she spent her time in the white rooms with all the equipment. They duplicated her body, showing her all of her bone structure and each minor bit of damage or change that had been done to it.

The machines ran non-invasive tests on every muscle in her frame, tracing their stress and the history of that slight price. They followed in reverse the wear and build-up of callous on her feet. One was a micro inch wider than the other, but both were unusually strong for a female.

It involved some invasion, but the trained personnel were quick and effective, and careful. They took swabs from her vagina, anal opening, mouth, nose, and ears. They had a robot nurse draw several tubes of blood with a needle she could barely feel.

At last, feeling she had no more secrets, she was told that everything was done from her side. But that was only the beginning. Her subsequent grueling sessions were with the statements she was required to fill in on her experiences with the gentleman called Blu Tho'Drik.

In that area was a special room, or several of them, as she was passed from interrogator to interrogator. These rooms had comfortable chairs for her to sit in across a table from the person who was asking the questions. Located everywhere were hidden cameras that caught everything. The rooms were kept at a comfortable heat, and the lights were normal to allow both the interrogator and the person sitting on the other side of the table to see each other.

Some of the people asking her the questions were those seeking to prosecute her stalker. Some were lawyers who would fight on Blu's side, primarily to prevent sending him for a long term. Some were neutral and for the courts. Others were only there to collect information, as Blu had unusual technology.

Behind the comfortable chair that they asked Kina to sit in was a special screen on the wall. No matter what she did, how she moved, where she placed her hands or legs, the chair read her and would tell if she lied. It was the best lie detector ever invented, as it read people's minds. It sent out tiny impulses constantly that fed to the brain and flowed back. The chair provided the information instantly to a large bank of computers in the wall behind the chair. All the millions of cells in the brain sitting in a chair were analyzed, and the truth was determined. It was never wrong, although many intelligent people had tried to fool it.

For weeks, Kina ate with other pilots and workers, got time out for exercise, was checked with the meds to make sure she was in good shape, and reported to the room daily.

It was on one of these trips as she was leaving that an escort was talking with her. "I guess your trips here are almost over."

Looking up, she saw that a part of the hall that was usually open had been blocked by temporary panels.

"What is that about?" Kina's nosy part of her system perked.

"Oh, they are getting ready to bring in the captive. They block off everything and don't take him out of his bubble until he is in the room."

The escort was moving away from her, so she turned away and quickly caught up.

Since he seemed to be talkative this time, she continued. "So, he talks in the chair?"

Her escort chuckled as he turned the corner to the outside door and a small floater cart was there to take her back to the boarding house.

"Talk. I have been able to watch some of the vids. There isn't much that is compromised by government information. He doesn't shut up. If the question is about our system, the man begins to give them full details of our entire system. He spends hours rattling off the exact amount of space, miles, and diameters of the entire area. He tells how many rocks of a particular size are in the outside Kuiper belt and then goes on to list the larger rocks on the main asteroid belt. This guy is too smart."

Listening to the young man in the lower grade Shayde uniform, she began to understand. "Does he say anything about himself?"

The guy laughed as he pulled up at the front door for the standard housing. "Nope. Drives them nuts as they hunt back through every word he mutters, hoping for one slip or mix-up. Nothing. This guy is smarter than us, and we may be in trouble." His last words were said with a frown as she got out of the cart.

Not wanting to be alone with the information she had now, she went to the bar and ordered a stiff drink. They waited for the decision of the court.

Chapter Fourteen

Blu Tho'Drik, a citizen of unknown places, was found guilty of stalking important personnel of a prominent corporation, putting a large number of traveling citizens in jeopardy, being in control of unique technology that was a danger to the Military, all Law Officials, and citizens. The prisoner was to be transferred to serve a life sentence in the maximum-security penal institution known as 5758 under Federated Military control.

That was the notice sent to Captain Kina Russel, as well as the notice that she was to report to duty. Getting into a clean new uniform that had been sent over with a tote full of the standard travel supplies, Kina saw that she was still a ship's captain for Shayde Transport.

Entering the large ship as she got off a shuttle in the big bay, again she was reminded of the size of the *Eclipse Shayde*. Still, as Kina walked up the steps to the long narrow hallway heading to the front of the ship, she felt almost at home. It seemed quiet, and she wondered if the crew had not come aboard yet.

It was at the galley where she knew she was in the right place.

"Welcome aboard, Captain." It was the pleasant voice of the AI Mark One coming from the eating area. Sitting at the table was Deak, with three tall mugs filled with something that looked suspiciously like beer. Briget was holding a large knife and looked like she was about to kill a cake that was near where she stood at the edge of the table.

"Welcome," echoed Deak. "It looks like one beer won't hurt as a homecoming drink. It seems we have a two-day lay-over while they begin to load up our deliveries."

"Yeah, boss. How about a piece of homemade cake?"

Briget began to slice the cake with the big knife. "They let me check out everything and then kicked me off. So I took baking lessons. Hope you guys like something that a machine didn't pop out."

With that, all three sat down and ate a delicious, too-sweet dessert and chased it down with one beer apiece. They spent a couple of hours catching up. Kina talked about all the time she spent in the truth chair, and Briget explained baking lessons. Deak said that there had been more weapons added to the *Eclipse,* so he had first studied them on vids and now had spent some time with hands-on experience.

At last, leaving her crew, Kina visited the bridge and then turned into her cabin for a long rest.

The next few days were busy while the team and Mark One checked out crew supplies and signed on delivery cartons. At last they were cleared for lift-off, and they headed for their first jump point.

After the third delivery, things had settled down, and life was becoming routine for the crew. Mark One was better than ever, setting up routes and watching for problems. On one jump, the AI passed on a warning from some ship's captains about interference from pirates. On Mark One's suggestion, they took a longer route and made the delivery only a short time later. The client was happy to get his cartons and didn't put on a late charge.

This time out was a short run, so they were gone for five weeks. The final delivery was on the return trip and a quick drop-off. Deak decided to take time to leave the ship, but Briget was going to stay on board to watch the unloading process. Kina was in her comfortable pilot's seat on the bridge and had most of the cameras up and running.

A minor glitch for the delivery on the side exit created a small problem. This time they had docked at a space station and had two door locks attached to the station as they snugged up sideways with their vast length. Closer to the front of the ship was the smaller exit for personnel, and back down the ship was a larger door lock that would handle big haulers and cartons. That was where Briget was working with the final delivery.

"Mark." Kina still had the habit of using only one word for the AI. "I'm having trouble with the camera on the side exit. We don't want someone trying to sneak onto the ship."

"On it, Captain. I have cameras working in that hallway in both directions, so we are safe. But perhaps we will need the engineer to check out the fuses in that area."

The AI must have been doing something, as Kina could see two screens blinking.

The inside screen came on and showed a clear view of the empty exit door lock. The outer camera blinked, and in an instant, Kina lost her breath. On the screen for a flicker was Blu's face with that wicked smile. Then it was gone, too fast for her to be sure as the screen cleared, showing the exit was clear, with people off in the distance in the landing area.

Leaning forward, she enlarged the view and moved the camera to see if anyone was running or the backs of anyone tall or large. "Mark, replay the screen that was blinking."

"Confirmed, Captain. How far would you like to see?" Mark began to scroll the screen back, and it soon showed only static.

"Halt. Go forward one frame at a time."

Kina watched as the AI controlled the screen. Blinks of grey and nothing but black interspersed, then it came on again, showing the open exit door.

Sitting back she realized she was breathing too fast. She was having a panic attack. Slowing her body down, she thought about what she'd seen in that split second. Was it something from her mind? Perhaps it was a vid caught for a split second from old files that were now wiped away. Would this strange male forever haunt her, even while he was locked up in the most secure military prison?

On the final return, they had a couple of days of rest as the big freighter traveled between jumps. In her cabin, Kina did some research on the maximum-security penal institution known as 5758 under Federated Military control.

The location was restricted and not on star maps. It was rumored to be in an asteroid belt and on a large, isolated rock that housed only the penal colony. The only safe approach was from a side away from the neighboring line of rocks and debris and by spaceship. It had huge automatic cannons triggered by approach that fired at anything. It was known to fire on loose asteroids that had slipped past.

Only the guards at the station could shut down the automatic system. The guards only had to serve duty at the colony for one year and were changed out by volunteers. Anyone who served as a guard at 5758 was given an upgrade in rank or moved closer to the end of their current release date. They all were Marines from the Federated Military.

The only schematic of the colony and the inside of the rock was old, something that had been proposed when the asteroid was changed from a mining development to a prisoner-holding area. The plan showed only one entrance, a square room that branched off to four more square rooms that then branched off to more square rooms. This was all inside the rock, as it was blasted away to hold the square shape of the exact shape of multiple ships' bays. These square areas from old ships were indestructible, as they were built to stand against whatever they had to hold and prevent damage from outer space.

Beyond the metal rooms was a large cavern that could hold hundreds of people and had floating lights. In this room, automatic systems managed the supplies of food, clothes, blankets, and some meds. Beyond that, the rock was a warren of caves, long mining shafts, and side chambers that went off into the dark.

One thing became a problem, because a few prisoners were kept in the metal rooms for their safety and the need of the Feds. But for the most part, it was everyone on their own in the rest of the area. It was rumored that there were fights and even riots. No guard entered the colony beyond the first room. But they did have the ability to send gas to knock out people in certain areas. Cameras were everywhere. It was a one-way prison. Once a person was sentenced to 5758, it was for life.

"Why is such a beautiful woman looking at something so ugly?" Deak's voice shocked Kina. She hadn't heard him board the ship and come up to the bridge. With his words, she quickly closed the screen down and turned the seat to face her crewman.

"Did you find anything good?" Kina motioned to the thin bag in his hand, trying to change the subject.

"Believe it or not, I got a pair of socks to sleep in. Supposed to keep your feet at the right temperature all night." He smiled and turned to go back to his cabin.

At least he brought a smile to her face, as she had to think about going onto a strange space station and buying socks.

"Captain, the engineer has a report," Mark announced quietly on a speaker in front of her seat.

"Please put her through." Kina had to wonder why Briget didn't use her wrist comm to make contact.

"Captain, the client who is accepting delivery of this last load has a request. He is here now on the outside loading dock. He has a large container to return to Salcap II. He is willing to pay a bonus because of not setting the paperwork up ahead of time. I'm sending you the info for you to forward to headquarters. I will wait for approval." Briget sounded very official, and Kina realized the client must be watching her.

"Mark, do we have a copy of all the information on that shipment that the customer wants to be sent back with us to the home zone?" Kina returned to face the dashboard and pulled up some special faceplates.

Everything looked correct, but it took over two hours to go through the system to get approval to accept the carton for shipment. Half of the payment was put into the ship's log, and at last, they were on their way home.

One of the things about being a captain or crew on a freighter was the fact that you were either very busy or had long hours of boredom. Kina didn't want to think about the hours of movies she had watched. She had read so many books, and she had a library full on her pad. Like her crew, she spent long periods working out, and then there was the time in the doc pod.

Everyone who spent so much time in space had to get into the pods to get their systems checked and cleaned from the contamination of what space was throwing at them all the time. Even with all the modern shielding, the nanites in their bodies, and the safety of the off-ship suits, there was still some penetration from space. At least in the pods, they were asleep, and time passed quickly.

As often as possible, the small crew ate their meals together and talked about the recent news they watched on the media. But there were times when Kina did appreciate being by herself, alone in her cabin with her thoughts. Time passed, and Mark One sent the announcement to everyone that they were coming out of the last jump. The three were back in the mode where they were busy and doing their jobs.

This was the central area of civilized worlds where the population was high, and more than planets were covered with homes and buildings.

Mark One and Captain Russel made constant contact with different controllers as they moved the big ship through one system after another. Crewman Deakon Warvel handled the shields and small screens that looked for vagrant contacts that could cause problems. Engineer Briget Blahx was deep in the side sector where the cores were buried, where she stood over a report board and babied her large machines through spurts of power.

At last, they were circling Salcap II, and the landing instructions were being followed. They sat down with hardly a bump to show the skill of its crew and AI. After a moment, the standard order for all door locks to open was given, and there was a shudder as the crew felt the action.

Starting to rise out of her seat, Kina heard a startling alarm, and she froze.

"Mark One, what is the problem?" Kina immediately started to hit the controls on some screens to see if they were being attacked.

"Captain, I have lost all cameras and sensors for Bay One." The AI's tone was a bit more mechanical than usual.

Chapter Fifteen

Hitting the button to shut off the alarm, Kina immediately sent out a call to security. She needed them to surround her ship and keep anyone away from that open bay door.

The next words were from Briget on the wrist comm. "Captain, I'm in the bay now, and the lid is off the last container, and it is empty."

"Lock everything down." Kina hit a special button that alerted security. It was a notice of contamination release. It would put the *Eclipse* automatically in isolation. It also got an immediate reaction from the local security, as lights flooded the landing zone and drones began to fill the air.

Armed land and floating vehicles were soon heading in the direction of the enormous freighter, as other ships near that location were also locked down. Because this was the home site, the number of soldiers that security could call up on short notice was extensive.

"Captain Russel?" The voice coming through the ship's speaker could be heard throughout the ship.

Punching a couple of buttons, Kina had control of the speakers and answered. "This is Captain Russel.

"I'm Lieutenant Gaston, in charge of the notice of your problem. We are sending in snifters. Please describe the situation."

"Lieutenant, we had one container still on board to drop off here for a client to pick up at the standard storage barn. Everything was normal until landing. After the shutdown of engines and standard opening of door locks, we lost all cameras in Bay One, where the container was stored. My engineer went to check on the camera situation and found the container open and empty. We have no detail of what the carton contained. We have no idea what might have been released when the lid was removed. The crew of three, my engineer, my second, and myself, can provide exact positions at the time of the incident." She stopped talking and waited for security to take over.

The crew was ordered to stay together on the bridge as equipment quickly assessed any threats. It took the snifters, outside cameras, and sensors, along with special security personnel, to determine there was no danger of anything that would harm individuals. Whatever was inside the carton was not leaving any harmful trace. In fact, from their equipment checks, the carton had been empty. What had popped the lid off was a good question.

Lieutenant Gaston released the crew, and the ship, as a security hauler took the carton and kept the bay under lockdown. As he was leaving, he notified Kina that she was to report to the head of security.

After getting a ride on a fast cart across the large landing zone, Kina had been looking forward to going to the hostel for the crew, but instead she was heading for security.

The Major was a no-frills man who had her escorted into his office as soon as she showed, even before dawn.

"Have a seat, Captain." The Major had several privacy screens up as Kina took a seat and saw only the plain back of the platforms. "You have had a very interesting life."

It looked like he had been reading something. Kina thought it was the latest report on the incident on her ship. His eyes focused on her, and he gave her a once-over that was almost a man-type of observation. She refused to feel uncomfortable. As a ship's captain, she had thrown off a lot of flirting glances.

"Is there a problem with the latest investigation, *Major*?"

Kina stressed the title to throw the conversation into a more professional mode.

"No, Captain, the report says the issue is strange, and security is going back to the original client. Everything checks out for you and your crew, and after they release the bay, they will begin to accept more stock for shipment." He glanced again at one screen.

"The reason I asked you to report to my office was about something different. It had to do with the court case you were involved in last year. I'm sure you remember the one involving a prisoner by the name of Blu Tho'Drik." It wasn't a question.

Kina wished she could see the screen that was hidden by the privacy shield. "With regrets, I remember that issue, Major."

"Well, a Universal notice has been sent out. It seems that Blu Tho'Drik has escaped from Five Seven Five Eight." The man behind the desk sat back after making such a shocking statement.

Unsure what she said or how she had even moved, sometime later, Kina was in a standard crew room in the hostel or hotel near the landing zone. It was owned by Shayde, Inc., and the crew stayed as long as they wanted at a very low cost.

All she could think about was how had that big man got out of the only place where no one had ever escaped before? So that one blink had been his face on the screen. Sinking on the soft couch, she had to shake her head in wonder. It was a handsome face, so why would such an unusual male, who had all those amazing tech supplies, be interested in her?

Yet now, he had been in her life for years, a hidden shadow that left her job at risk. She had a week before she could report to the *Eclipse,* and she hated every hour away from the ship. Kina expected each wrist call or pad alert to have those unusually blue eyes looking at her. Every dark street and shadow in the room gave her chills as she expected to see the movement of that large muscular body.

But finally, there was the notice that the freighter was cleared for travel. With her travel tote and in a new fresh uniform, Kina was escorted over to the *Eclipse* by a junior security guard. In the daylight, she could see the new paint or relatively thin metal coating that had been applied to the ship. It made her look like new, even though she was an odd-shaped spaceship.

Uniformed guards were spaced around the *Eclipse,* but it was not the only ship with protection. All the ships on the landing zone had the sight of guards moving on foot or in floating carts. Shayde, Inc. had the whole place on alert, even though an escaped prisoner from a penal colony was so far away and in a different system.

Getting into the side door lock and looking back at all the people working to protect all that Shayde owned, Kina had to wonder if they weren't looking at the wrong place. With all the extra checks, it took longer to load the freighter, and the crew was informed they would be taking on more shipments at their different stops.

The first delivery was frozen food in several containers to a moon that was settled by domes. It was a long distance that involved several jumps. Any spaceship was still limited by the laws of physics and could not travel faster than the speed of light in normal space. But with the core jump engine installed and finding a local spot in space that had an unusual twist in it, things could change. Between the core engine and the special twist in space, a ship would go from one location to another, and uncounted billions of miles were instantly crossed. It seemed that a spaceship was traveling faster than light.

The boring long nights meant no sleep for a captain that worried about an escaped prisoner. Kina spent hours in the small area where mats and exercise equipment were available. Mark One had a small drone or cameras on her all the time as a backup for any apparatus that might suddenly go down. But other than restless nights and two worried crew personnel about their boss, the freighter made its way uneventfully to a settled moon that desperately needed food.

Because of the size of the freighter and no real landing zone, Kina had to get into the large shuttle and transport loads down to the assigned reception area. It was inside an oversized garage that could have the atmosphere removed for small ships to enter. Once the doors were sealed, the air was returned, and people and haulers would go to work.

In the shuttle on the third and last delivery, Kina had the large hauler, with Mark One able to communicate through the machine with her. They had six large cold cartons to unload, and they were not picking up anything from the sad colonized location.

Riots were taking place, and in the area where they were unloading her cargo, there were armed guards. But she could still hear the sounds of people fighting and yelling that seemed to be coming closer. It wasn't a space that could be protected easily, as it was a large bubble attached to several other air-controlled bubbles that led down underground.

Hoping to get the last containers off the shuttle quicker, Kina was riding the back of her large hauler, which had a carton on it heading across the floor, when all hell broke loose. Suddenly there were hundreds of people coming across the floor from all directions. Now she could hear gunfire.

Hordes of desperate hungry-looking people poured through all the entrances and trampled the guards. They soon reached the cartons and began to tear at them, pushing the hauler and Kina over. From the floor, she saw only legs. Trying to crawl backward to the shuttle, she heard Mark One calling up to the *Eclipse*. As she froze in horror at the dirty, hungry people, a strong arm wrapped around her, and suddenly she was up on her feet against a warm wall from behind.

"Hello, sweetheart."

She felt the voice through her back against him. Around her, a large hand slugged a ragged man who was charging them. The fist connected, and the man flew back off his feet and took two more with him. At that, another took a look at Kina and whoever was holding her, and decided the metal food containers looked better.

Pushing against the arm that felt like a metal bar holding her, she realized they were moving backward as she watched the crowds fighting each other in the chaos. The shock of seeing people fighting and now killing over food left her limp as he pulled her further away from the scene and her lost hauler.

"We've reached your shuttle, beautiful. Can you stand now?"

His voice was like a drum in his chest. He was so wide and tall that his head was above hers.

"Are you going to kill me now?" Kina felt the arm loosen, and she stood upright to take a step away. She took a breath after her question and couldn't decide if she wanted to turn her back on the wild scene of the crowd or the killer. She settled on only a bit of a half step sideways and looked up at him. There were those unusual eyes and, of course, that wicked smile. Then behind him, only a couple of feet away, was the ramp to her shuttle.

"You want my shuttle too?" She frowned at him. "I should have armed myself. I'm so stupid." But she jumped at a loud noise behind her. The crowd had found a way to break into a carton. It brought a cheer from some.

"Oh, baby. I save that pretty ass, and all I get is a frown. Not only that…"

He reached out, and before she could even draw back, he

was so quick he had her by the upper arms. The hold hurt a little, but what he was doing was shifting her around to stand on the bottom of the ramp.

"I have my ship. But I would settle for a thank you or, better, a kiss." One dark eyebrow rose on his broad forehead.

"I'd rather find a knife to stick in your heart, if I could find your heart." She took a careful step backward to see if he was going to let her get away. But she needed to ask one question as long as she was facing him.

"Why are you making my life so miserable? Why are you following me?" She had to nearly shout, to be heard over the noise as frozen food was being tossed about.

"Because of what happened here. You are too reckless, and I'm meant to keep you safe. Besides, why wouldn't a man want to watch over a beautiful woman?"

She could see that frightful smile again.

"So, do I get a smile or, better, a kiss? I have been told I can give a lady a lot of pleasure with one kiss."

Why was his voice so soft but still able to carry over the noise of the fighting in the background?

"Touch me again, and I will knee you in that ego." She looked him up and down as she took steps backward. He might be a giant of a man, but he still had all the right parts. All women were trained in the art of self-protection, maybe because they were known to be weaker.

The last she saw of him was the smile and his head shaking as she slammed her hand against the red emergency button that forced the ramp and door quickly closed.

Chapter Sixteen

Captain Kina Russel didn't have a stalker—she had a so-called admirer. What the hell was going on in her life? Kina spent a short time in the doc pod at the insistence of her crew.

Coming out of the pod feeling more refreshed than she wanted, Kina joined Deak and Briget in the galley to get caught up on the ship's business.

"We got the ship out and onto the next route. Mark One is helping with the navigation." Briget sat a thick drink in front of Kina. "Also, the engines are in good shape. We are up and running at top speed."

"I reported to headquarters about the loss of the big hauler," Deak said as he reached for the same type of drink. Briget was still trying out her cooking school concoctions.

"But," Deak added. "Mark One is in mourning over the loss of one of its children. We need to replace the large hauler to help it get over the sadness you will hear in the speakers."

Looking up at a speaker, Kina asked for a report. "Mark, did you record the incident with my stalker and the chaos over the food on the landing zone?"

"Affirmative, Captain." The voice was male but low in pitch. "I uploaded everything from the large hauler until we were too far away for contact. I also had complete vids of you and the male that saved you and helped you to the ramp of the shuttle. The cameras, both inside and outside the shuttle, ran the entire time. Also, the cameras on the *Eclipse* had records of the shuttle returning, and another small dark ship leaving the moon at the same time. It disappeared immediately."

"Wait!" Kina pushed away the health drink as she took in the information Mark One was giving her. "You got a clear picture of the male that grabbed me at the ramp of the shuttle?"

"Affirmative, Captain." The voice was from the single speaker in the ceiling over the table. The AI had several choices in the room, but had chosen that one, allowing everyone to hear.

Kina was gripping the edge of the table. "You also got a good vid of his ship? Please tell me you got a camera shot of the ship that can give us some details."

"Affirmative, Captain." There was a pause. "When and where would you like to view the vids, Captain?"

Deak was right, as Kina took in the AI's words. Mark was acting a little different, not as friendly, more like an AI that didn't know the crew as a friend.

"I need to get to the bridge. We need to get in contact with home security." Kina was up and moving fast, up the narrow hallway to get up through the door lock and into the bridge.

"Mark," Kina called out as she slid into her favorite seat. The pilot's chair immediately began to shift and fit comfortably around her body. Most modern seats and chairs were built to move and adjust to the body that sat in it, but for some reason, Kina felt this pilot's seat felt even better.

"Ready, Captain." The AI voice coming from the small speaker in front of her on the dashboard now sounded more like the old AI who had become part of her crew. Perhaps it was because she had called it by just Mark.

"First, we need to get copies of anything concerning the damage and loss of the large hauler. We also need to duplicate and send anything that has the vid of Blu Tho'Drik, and the ship you caught leaving the moon at the same time that my shuttle left. We want to make sure that nothing happens to those records. This guy has the habit of performing technological miracles, and I don't want to lose our records." She sat back for a second, trying to think through to make sure she had not missed anything about what Mark had recorded.

By this time, Deak was in his seat beside her and was also sending out messages to headquarters and security. He was a smart and efficient man and was taking the proper steps.

"Mark." Deak gave his orders knowing the AI was capable of working with both of them and several others without a problem. "Bring up the vid of the ship that left the moon at the same time we did. I need to do some intense scrutinizing." He had a large screen above him that he was pulling down, and a dark view began to run.

With her fingers busy filling in the forms on what had happened on the moon from the first encounter of problems, Kina glanced over now and then at the dark screen Deak was working with. He would stop the vid now and then and enlarge a portion of the small black spaceship.

"Damn."

His harsh word broke into Kina's concentration. "What?" She looked over at a strange picture on the screen that didn't make any sense.

"Your friend has been hired by some very expensive corporation that is providing him with top-grade equipment." Deak was enlarging something even more, and she could see some engraving in metal. "That part is a prototype of a fin that is not even in production yet. It is for future military use for the Feds."

"How does a guy get a part on his ship that isn't even in production?" Kina went back to filling in the long reports needed on the loss of the hauler.

"How does he escape from a prison that no one else has ever gotten away from?" Deak began to move the image on the screen. "Why would some corporation that is bigger and richer than most governments hire a guy to follow you?"

Deak had now caught her attention enough that she stopped typing and sat back to think and stare at his dark screen. "Why indeed? Have you watched the vid where he captures me?"

"No. Let's look at it now." Deak flipped something up on the largest screen above their heads and over the transparent window. He fast-forwarded until he had a view from the shuttle ramp of a large body that was holding Kina off the ground.

"Hello, sweetheart." They watched as he slugged a ragged man who was charging them, sending him flying back off his feet and taking two more with him.

"Gods, that man is fast." Deak commented and continued watching the screen as another person showed up, took one look at Kina and whoever was holding her, and turned away to the food. The large body was shielding Kina, and apart from her kicking legs, most of her body could not be seen by the shuttle's camera. The man pulled her further away from the scene and her lost hauler.

Kina's discomfort rose as she continued watching herself.

"We've reached your shuttle, beautiful. Can you stand now?" The man was so wide and tall that his head was above hers in the vid.

Kina now heard her own shaky voice. *"Are you going to kill me now?"*

At last, the camera showed her ability to step away. The vid showed her taking a small step to the side and looking up at him, then behind him toward her shuttle ramp.

Both Deak and Kina looked closely at the screen that showed their ramp on their own shuttle.

"You want my shuttle, too?"

The screen showed her frowning at him. *"I should have armed myself. I'm so stupid."*

But the vid then showed her jerking, and they could hear a loud noise behind her. The screen exposed the rioters, who'd found a way to break into a carton and were cheering.

They watched Kina's focus shift to the crowd, but his words brought her back to him. *"Oh, baby. I save that pretty ass and all I get is a frown. Not only that..."*

The next scene drew a shudder from her—moving faster than their vision could track, the man suddenly held her by her arms and placed her to stand on the bottom of the ramp. *"I have my ship. But I would settle for a thank you or, better, a kiss."* The camera on his face picked up the one dark eyebrow rise on his broad forehead.

Kina shifted on her seat, wishing she was watching this alone. Her next words on the vid were nearly shouting, easy to hear over the chaos in the background.

"I'd rather find a knife to stick in your heart if I could find your heart." The vid showed her taking a step backward, closer to the shuttle. *"Why are you making my life so miserable? Why are you following me?"*

Deak glanced over at Kina as if he was also asking the same question.

"Because of what happened here. You are too reckless, and I'm meant to keep you safe. Besides, why wouldn't a man want to watch over a beautiful woman?"

The close up showed his face smiling. *"So, do I get a smile or, better, a kiss? I have been told I can give a lady a lot of pleasure with one kiss."* His voice was soft but seemed to carry over the noise of the fighting in the background also.

Kina was surprised the camera had so clearly picked up what he said—when he'd spoken those words, she'd felt them more as a rumble in her body alone. She wished she could skip some of her next comments on the rerun.

"Touch me again, and I will knee you in that ego."

The vid showed her looking him up and down as she took careful steps backward up the ramp. Once inside, she slammed the emergency button closing the ramp and the door and ending the vid.

neither Deak nor Kina spoke for long minutes. She was in shock, and he appeared to be mystified.

"Another corporation as big as Shayde or bigger?" Deak finally mumbled, more focused on the technology than on what Kina had endured or her reactions.

"Did you hear what that asshole said to me?" Kina sat back in a huff.

Looking over at her, Deak grinned. "Well, it is better to have a guy that likes you than one that wants to hurt you. That guy is a monster of muscle and could win in one of the Tournament of Champions on any night. Come on, Boss, you are a beautiful woman, so why wouldn't he be interested?"

Glancing over at her fellow crewman, Kina was surprised at his comment. Up until this time, none of the three had engaged in any flirting or shared any emotions, even though they were closed up together on the ship for long periods. She'd never had any idea Deak saw her as anything but a captain and a crewmember. His use of the word *beautiful* left her feeling strange.

Almost as strange as those unusually blue eyes on the very tall male who had recently held her. She shook her head as she tried to get the thought of Tho'Drik out of her mind. Was it true? Was he a hired gun sent to follow her? If there was a big corporation behind him, that would explain his escape from 5728. It would take a lot of help and some bribes to get a man out of that penal colony.

Pushing aside the forms she was filling in, she brought up a general search file. Seeking the largest universal corporations was easy, but that led to a long list of company names, and it was in alphabetical order. Kina tried again, limiting the list to the top one hundred largest corporations sorted by maximum worth. Shayde was not on this list, and she found she didn't recognize most of the company names.

Two of the corporations that were down on the list were connected with transportation or shipping. Kina recognized the names from seeing the ships in different ports. Another entry was a big surprise—a group of independent shippers that had formed a union called Democratic Shippers Universal.

Because it was different and unusual, Kina clicked on it, and the screen began to scroll with tons of information. The DSU was an organization of independent shippers. It listed many lawsuits, several of which the DSU had won in court decisions. The regular corporate shippers weren't happy with the independents. The suits were about prices, routes, clients, and contracts, and the DSU won them all, costing the appellants massive amounts in court costs and settlements.

A smile came across Kina's face as she cleared the screen. So the underdog was often a winner. Perhaps that was a message for her and her tormentor. She went back to filling in the final reports to send back to headquarters about the fiasco at the moon delivery.

The following two deliveries, including one pickup, went off with no problems. The crew stayed on board, with the captain in her seat and Mark One having all cameras working. The next delivery was a long trip with three jumps, so Kina spent a lot of restless nights in her cabin and long hours in the exercise area.

Even with the good food Briget was creating, Kina ate little, as her appetite was for coffee only. They were in between the first and last jump for the delivery, and the AI announced they had a contact coming through.

Kina was in the bay jogging and stopped. "Hold it until I reach the bridge."

Grabbing a small towel and keeping up her jogging motion, Kina hurried through the bay, up the ladder, and down the long narrow hallway. She continued running past the cabins and the galley and finally up the short way through the door lock to the bridge. Getting into the pilot's seat, she wiped the sweat off with the rag and hit a couple of buttons.

"Ready, Mark."

"Confirmed, Captain. Audio and video on your prime screen."

What she saw was a grey streak and static, and when the screen cleared, Kina sucked in a breath. Blu was staring back at her from his bridge.

"Damn, Mark, close off the contact." Kina was furious. How had he gotten through to her ship?

"Wait, Sweetheart. This is important." He seemed to lean into the camera.

"Calling me trite words is not a way to tell me something is important." She put her hand up to show him she was about to disconnect them.

There was silence for a moment, and then her curiosity got away from her. "Okay, what is so important?"

Chapter Seventeen

"Listen carefully, babe. I'm sending proof of what I'm telling you. You don't want to make the next stop. It is a trap, with some mercenaries who have paid off the locals." He seemed to be looking down, and Mark One did a beep of receiving vids and info.

Another screen lit up and showed several ships standing just inside the exit from the jump site. The space station was dark with no activity around it, not even any docking ships.

"Mark, plot a course that will take us to the following delivery. It will take us off course. Use override code." Kina took a minute to glance at her wrist comm. On it, she had already pulled up some information and sent an alarm out to Deak. "The code is KR One, Three Two Two Four."

"Confirmed, Captain."

Mark now had its better voice in place, and she could feel movement in the ship. Kina knew Briget would be contacting her any second.

Looking back at the face on the screen in the pilot's position, she nodded. "Your information has been certified. Uh, why are you doing this? Helping us. I mean, thanks."

A noise blared behind her, and Deak was leaning over her seat so he could examine the screens. It was a lot to take in for the crewman, but he was smart and had a lot of time out in the deep dark and quickly saw the problem.

"Damn," was his only word. At last, he bent down to look over her shoulder at the man's face on the screen.

"We need to meet on AuPa. That is your next stop,

gorgeous. I have a proposition. Well, I have two, one is a business idea, and the other is personal." With his last words, that wicked grin was back on his face.

Kina snorted as she reached a hand forward. "You can take your proposal and shove it up your ass." She was about to shut off the contact when Deak caught her wrist.

"I think you should meet with him. After all, he did save us a big problem with the mercenaries waiting on the other side of the jump gate."

Kina looked at Deak almost face to face. He had a serious expression on him. "Okay, but we must meet in a public place." Saying the words to Deak, Kina knew that it was being picked up by the contact with Blu.

Because of the change of direction, they were confined to the ship for a longer time. Deak made some inquiries and set up the meeting for Kina and Blu at a local bar that was close to the docking area on the space station. The space station was located above a beautiful colonized planet, and transport from the station to the planet was via a tethered line. Kina was grateful that Deak was smart enough to find the bar on the station so that she'd be close to the freighter and wouldn't have to take the long trip down to the planet.

Any of them, including Kina, would have loved to spend some time on the planet AuPa, since it was a lovely agricultural world with oceans and beaches. But Briget was angry at the misuse of her pampered engines, and Deak was working on getting messages back to headquarters. Kina was angry and worried about sitting in a bar with her nemesis.

Though jumps were always fast, the next few seemed slow to Kina, and timed dragged by. Kina spent restless nights and hours jogging with too much coffee in her system.

Briget worked on her engines and tried out new recipes. The smell of good food drifted through the ship, even down to the large holds. Deak checked out the different weapons systems, sent additional reports back to headquarters, and checked general messages. They were too far out to get any fast quantum reports until they made contact at AuPa.

Finally they exited the last jump and moved through normal space. Kina was at her place, and she and Mark were in control of slowing the ship to make the docking maneuvers.

The unloading at AuPa was going to take longer, as cartons had to be shifted. Some containers should have been taken off at the previous stop, but they'd skipped that appointment because of the mercenaries. Now all those packing cases had to be either moved out or shifted aside to bring out the cases that were noted for AuPa.

The large planet needed a lot of small mechanical parts that came in heavy containers, and the *Eclipse* was short one large hauler, so they had to rely on haulers from the dock area. That meant waiting for haulers to be available and then having either Deak or Briget oversee their use and movements.

Because they were both in the process of unloading, Kina was on her own to go off the ship and meet with the big man she labeled obnoxious. It took her a long time to get ready, and when she was done, she realized she had gone out of her way to hide her looks and her body. She wasn't sure if it was the need to be safe or to be concealed from those strange eyes.

Along with heavy black baggy military pants with many pockets, she wore a black tee shirt under a thick matching jacket. Within the pockets and in the heavy boots, she hid small knives, gas propellants, and small metal tools. She smiled, as she knew she would not be able to pass through a metal detector. But there weren't any on the station, except when passengers queued up to descend to the planet.

With her hair tucked back under a simple knit cap and no make-up, she nodded at her image in the mirror in the bathroom. She had two hours before locating the bar and meeting with the person who had almost ruined her life.

Getting to the bar early allowed her to find a table near the rear where she could watch the people enter. It was a busy but quiet place, with the music soft enough to let people talk. The waiter was an efficient robot that worked with a live barman behind the long waist-high counter along one side of the room.

The quiet room was suddenly silent as a prominent figure filled the doorway and made a perfect dark shadow from the outside light. Kina felt a kick in her stomach. Was it fright, or something else? Refusing to find anything about this absurd man attractive, she froze while he approached.

If he looked around, he did it without turning his head as he made his way direct to her table. In her mind, she thought perhaps he had used some of those fancy gadgets to see her location before coming into the room. Perhaps Deak was correct, that he was a hired gun for some rich company, some competitor of *Shayde.* Well, he wouldn't learn any secrets about the shipping or the company from her. She gritted her teeth and clutched the coffee mug. She was grateful the bar hadn't hesitated when she ordered coffee instead of alcohol.

Turning the chair around, he sat on it and put his arms on the back to face her across the small table.

Kina now wished the bar had larger tables. With a flutter deep in her stomach as she felt him looking at her so intently, she swallowed.

The table's menu lit up for him to order, and he swiped something swiftly as if to get it out of the way. "You need sleep, sweets?"

Blu spoke quietly, but Kina was aware that most of the people around them were glancing over at him. He did attract attention. Those broad shoulders blocked out most of the room behind him from her view.

"Are you a cyborg? Your size and muscles are not the norms." Kina decided to try to be the aggressor. She hated when he called her those cute names.

"Genetically altered in youth. Does that create a bias in you? I am still all man, especially in one important part." He raised an eyebrow with that last couple of words.

"Damn, what is wrong with your ego. I'm in trouble with my employer, my friends, and everything I consider important, and you are acting like you have a woman out on a date. You don't have any…" She ran out of words.

"I'm sorry for your pain, my beauty. My main job is to protect you from all harm, and I am truly sorry for any pain I have caused you."

His voice was so soft it was like a breeze coming across the table.

At that moment, the robot waiter rolled up a large mug of beer and carefully placed it in front of Blu.

Blu ignored it as he watched her closely and continued speaking, so softly Kina knew no one else in the busy bar would hear. "You are an exceptional pilot. You are among the highest-paid pilots by Shayde, but there are other opportunities out there for you that are better for someone with your abilities. Shayde is taking advantage of your talents."

"Oh, no, no, no." Kina was shaking her head. "This is where you make an offer of a bribe for me to give information on routes or ships. Damn, damn, damn." She couldn't see the door behind his large body, but she could always run toward the bar.

"Don't be foolish." Blu grinned. "Before you are out of that chair, I will have you in my arms, and I will enjoy it. Now don't panic. I am not offering you a stupid bribe. Why would we present such a thing to someone as smart as they are gorgeous? No, I'm talking about you owning your ship." He picked up the beer and took a long drink, taking almost half of the full mug.

Kina was glad that Blu was distracted from drinking the

beer, as it gave her a chance to sit and think about what he was saying and what the words meant. What exactly *was* he saying? What did he mean about her owning a ship? Then she put two and two together and decided he might be working for Democratic Shippers Universal.

Glad that he wasn't saying anything more, as he was slugging down the beer, Kina realized she knew very little about the DSU. She'd seen ships that were not affiliated with any company delivering or picking up cargo on different sites. She'd never paid any attention to them any more than she looked at the other companies' ships that were docked nearby. Questions?

Chapter Eighteen

A strange idea ran through her head. What would it be like to have the freedom to own her ship, to be the real boss? To not have those long reports to fill out before and after each delivery, not to always have someone else decide where you were going? How much freedom did the people that belonged to the DSU have with their ships?

"So, I've got you thinking about being a pilot. Maybe you will think about what it will feel like to spend the night with a real man." With that, he stood and slowly walked out, leaving Kina with more problems than ever.

Why did this huge handsome male cause so much disruption in her life? There had to be some dark secret behind the whole problem if someone had hired him to help her, as he'd said. That didn't make any sense.

Knowing that she needed to get back to the ship and talk this over with her friends, she swiped the bill on the table, and it showed paid. "How the hell does he do those things?" She left the bar to make her way back to the docks. Fortunately, the bar was close to the dock area, and her ID got her through the different pass gates.

The mess in the delivery seemed to have been straightened out, and Mark One was controlling the rented large hauler. Thanks to the agreement, they only had to set the containers out on the dock where the client was making arrangements to move them down on the elevator thread. They were appreciated for use on the planet below.

While Briget got the extra cartons strapped down for the

return trip home, Deak came forward to get a report from Kina.

As they grabbed coffee in the galley, Kina sat in one of the chairs, and Deak made them sandwiches. To her surprise, she felt she could eat something.

"So, did he threaten you or try something odd?" Deak worked on the sandwiches as he glanced over his shoulder at his captain.

"No. He paid for our drinks in one of his mysterious ways. The guy is full of secret tricks."

Nodding, Deak was now in his seat and bringing up the bay camera where Briget was having a problem with one of the cartons.

"Deak." Kina was again searching for information on her screen. "Did you know that the Democratic Shippers Universal group is more prominent and more prosperous than Shayde?"

"That's amazing. I do see their ships wherever we dock. They seem to be everywhere on the outer rim and less traveled routes. I bet you never saw one when you were in that fancy passenger ship." Deak was busy checking something on his dashboard as he spoke.

"I don't think I would have known what the DSU initials meant, even if I'd seen one." Kina had gotten past all the court action and was finally into factual information about the history of DSU.

"Not letters or words, Boss. They only have a big red handprint that looks like someone dipped their palm in paint and slapped the side of the ship. It always has drips coming down in red, and above the first finger is a red fingerprint. Go out into the docking area here and walk along it. I bet you'll see more DSU ships with the handprint than any fancy freighters like ours from corporations. Be careful, though. There'll be a couple of mercenary ships out there that can be trouble."

At this point, Kina had found some real information about the DSU and what it was about, and how it had started. According to history, the original group was called Strapp & Langness United and consisted of about twenty or more ships and their owners who had agreed to form a union to help each other make connections and set up contracts. It was to format deliveries out on the fringe, where shipping was needed but routes were sparse and dangerous.

The original idea was that traveling with more than one ship at a time protected against the desperate marauders who played upon helpless single ships. Whenever two or three ships traveled together, they shared the profits. Then a third man entered the picture. His name was Majias, and he was retired from a large corporation, having been forced out because of his advanced ideas. He was traveling through the fringe with his ship and a large bank account with a lot of anger at the corporations that shut out the little companies. He also felt that because the big guys had control, ordinary families were now paying too much for necessities.

He had put a lot of his money into arming his ship and, in anger, found an open can of red paint in the dock area. He dipped his hand into it and slapped the side of his hand on the nose of his weaponized spaceship. *Give me a reason to use these weapons,* the history quoted him as saying as he then put his fingerprint above his first finger. *That is for justice.*

According to the records, he offered his ship as protection for anyone who would pay a fee of two percent of their profit. But the surprise was that it was a one-time fee, and they could call on him and his ship for one year any time they needed him.

His first contract and trip out enabled him to eliminate the largest pest in one sector, and word got around. People who owned their freighters began to sign up with him. As the money poured in and Majias needed help, more armed ships were developed and hidden out where the Feds didn't go to protect lone travelers.

It grew in leaps and bounds. It was a hole that needed to be filled, and these independent owners were the perfect fit. At first, it was the three men who ran things in a wildcat manner, but eventually, as word spread and more and more indies added their 2%, the Strapp & Langness United needed to become organized.

First, it became apparent that everyone that was paying the two percent had added the red hand to the nose of their ship. They now had a logo. So when Majias passed away from unknown causes, he left all of his inheritance to Strapp & Langness United, which now needed an office and a staff.

As long as they were setting up everything officially, they changed the name and called for an election. It grew as more indies joined. Many corporate pilots left their positions, took their bonus funds, and got a loan from DSU to purchase their freighter.

According to records, the DSU ships had the best record of on-time delivery and no problems with lawless interference. For reasons the media could not explain, DSU ships, with their famous red hand, were less interfered with on travels than any other corporate ships in operation. Now DSU, as a group and with its investments, was larger than most freight and passenger corporations.

Sitting back in her seat, Kina looked out the front window, from which she could see several ships in the docking area. "Have you ever talked to any of the DSU people? I mean, one of the captains or owners?"

"Sure, they're good people. However, don't get in a poker game with them. They'll end up with all of your money." Deak ended that statement with a laugh. "But then they'll pick up the bar bill and get you a cab ride back to your ship.

Yep, they are good people."

"Since Briget is still working, I'm going to stretch my legs." Getting out of the freighter was easy, as there were many door locks, but Kina chose the one near the nose, which led directly into the busy section of the docking area. It was wide and full of people, haulers of all sizes, and stacks of cartons and containers. Everything seemed to either be moving in a hurry or stuck in a line going nowhere.

Since she was only browsing, Kina stayed close to the front of the ships. Surprisingly, after she passed a corporate ship next to hers, she found a ship with a red hand on the nose of the ship. It didn't seem to be busy, so the crew must already be off board. The next ship also had a red hand on it and was busy, so she stepped away to avoid getting in their way. As she stepped out into the main walkway, she could see the shapes of a couple more ships, and they all had the red hand on them.

"Nice sight, sweets?"

It took everything in her nerves to keep from showing any reaction to having the big man lean down and whisper into her ear. Kina wasn't sure what he was talking about, but he might be referring to the number of ships with the red hand on them. Perhaps she could get some factual information from him. Walking out of the way of traffic and moving slowly towards the nearest ship, she felt him move with her. He was so close she could feel his body heat, and there was a small stir in her body. She refused to allow herself to feel any attraction to this monster.

"So, do you know any of the people from the independent ships?" Kina noticed a couple of workers on the ramp of the ship they were approaching.

"I know some people from almost any ship." Blu stepped to the side and nodded to the workers. They had stopped whatever it was they were doing and looked as if they were now guarding the ramp to their ship. These people did not take any chances on the dock area. But Blu reached out, and with both hands fisted, he knocked two intruders together, one on top of the other.

The three guards looked at each other, and one man stepped forward. He repeated Blu's strange motion, slamming a fist onto the other. With that, he returned to his friends, and they ignored Kina and Blu as they finished their job.

Taking a few steps away from the ramp and the work team, Kina continued her search for information. "So, you know the secret mode of saying hello to the DSU?"

"If you are going to travel alone a far distance from central, my beauty, it helps to know how to say hello to a lot of different people." He was moving step by step with her, almost as if they were attached. How could he move those long legs to match hers?

At this point, a group of well-dressed people in a variety of uniforms came out, laughing and pushing through. They were having a good time and must have been out together to either eat or, more likely, drink. As Kina and her shadow watched with interest, the group began to hug and say goodbyes. Getting closer as the group broke up, Kina noticed that some of the suits had expertly embroidered a red hand high on the left chest.

"Some of them are advertising that they belong to the Democratic Shippers Universal." She couldn't keep her shock from her voice.

"It surprises you that crews from different ships get together to have a good time when they are docked? When was the last time you met up with the crew from another Shayde ship and had a night out or met to sleep over? Fuck, Sweetheart, when was the last time you relaxed when on a delivery route and even had a nice conversation with someone not from your ship?"

He leaned close and gently put a hand on her waist. "When was the last time you met up with a man in a strange hotel and had a hot night to let you smile the next morning? I promise you I will leave you with a smile all the next day." His breath was now hot on her neck.

It took her a second to open her eyes and remember that she hated this man. She pulled away sharply. "You need that mouth sewed shut."

His answer was a short chuckle, but then he was gone. Turning quickly, she didn't have to be told that he had stepped away from her. She felt the cool breeze as the heat of his big body left her. Standing there, close to the ship, with the red hand on the nose of the ship, she watched the people passing. Most of them looked untroubled and seemed to have a purpose as they talked among themselves and waved to distant workers. It was a more relaxed way of working and returning to their ships than what she was used to with Shayde crews or other corporate workers.

Turning but staying out of the main busy transit area, Kina began to walk back towards her ship, which was further than she realized. She thought about the difference and knew some of it was due to the time clock. Everything on a corporate ship was by rules and times set by someone else, and the crew had to meet these deadlines. Kina supposed that a member of the DSU had to meet certain deadlines, but they probably set their own as they negotiated their contracts.

As a corporate crew, there were deductions of pay and bonuses that were eliminated for any infraction. Someone was always over you, watching, checking, and finding fault. It seemed they often looked more for errors than they did for excellence.

Why did that irritating big guy get her thinking about these strange ideas?

"Damn, I hate him," were the words she mumbled. But she rubbed her neck where his breath had touched, and a small smile touched her lips. "Damn."

Chapter Nineteen

Back on the *Eclipse,* Kina went to the bay to get her mind off everything that had happened in the dock area. Instead, she ran into a problem that underscored the primary thought Blu had triggered.

On the floor, Briget was cussing as she was adding additional tie-downs to the containers they were going to take back home. It was the items they couldn't deliver because marauders had set up a trap at that delivery location.

"Hey, Captain. I'm almost done here. You know we all are going to get a dot against our grade for taking these back. Too bad, because it would have been worse if the pirates had taken everything we had on board. Damn office asses, what do they know what goes on out here?" Briget hooked the last metal snap and nodded. "Done."

"Great." The word was almost a snarl from Kina as she turned to go up to the bridge. It was time to return to headquarters. But it was a long trip with a lot of time to think, something Kina wasn't looking forward to on the nights in her bunk.

Arriving at home to the standard landing zone, the crew was notified to report to Security Headquarters immediately. They were to bring their personnel pads, and the captain was to bring the ship's log. For Kina, this reinforced the feelings that Blu had raised in her about the faults of corporations and central organizations.

After spending hours in the freighter bringing it in for the landing, they were separated, and Kina found herself in a room with a couple of security officers for six more hours. Finally she had announced that she was going to piss in their chair if they didn't give her a break.

Finally she and her crew were released to their standard hotel rooms but told not to leave the area.

After a week, Kina got a notice that the ship was ready for its next several deliveries. The problem was that she didn't want to go on this trip. In the past, she had always looked forward to being in the pilot's seat and going out into the starlit space. But now it all felt different, under the control and dictates of the corporation.

One of the first things she decided she would do after taking the big freighter off to the jump gate was to write her resignation. This was going to be her last trip for the Shayde Corporation. Kina felt she was in an impossible situation. She did not want anything to do with Blu Tho'Drik and all the strange ideas he put into her head. But she also didn't want to be a pilot for Shayde Corporation with no future. Surely there was something else out there for her. She had considerable savings tucked away because she never wasted any funds on all the stops where she had visited.

Unlike other members of her crew, she didn't drink heavily or gamble. Her vices were minimal, merely buying a few clothes now and then and improving her personal pad. The full bonus she'd received from the Federated Service was still untouched. Most of the larger wages she had received when she was a passenger ship pilot were also piled up in a Universal Bank. Even the wages she now earned as a freighter pilot and put into another account on Salcap II were all there. She hardly spent any of her funds.

When she finished this trip, she could purchase a ticket on any ship and start on her own. She might even be able to discover some of the secrets that were out in the deep dark. Kina smiled as she thought that when she quit Shayde, the big guy would no longer be interested in her. She would not have any corporate information, like routes or what containers were going to a special location.

The first stops were without any interruptions, but Kina found her two friends seemed to be very quiet. Briget did not do any cooking but spent all of their long days in standard space back in engineering. Deak would share a mug of coffee with Kina, then disappear into different sections of the ship, mumbling about checking weapons or special settings.

It seemed they were a ship of strangers, bored with the long days of waiting for the next jump position. To top it all off, Mark One, the AI, had turned back to the metallic voice and seemed in a depression. Could an AI get in a depression?

It was as Kina sat looking out the window of the freighter at their next stop that she saw the ship that was slowly docking beside them. It was slowly coming in, and for a short time, Kina had a view of the nose with the red hand painted on the nose. The first finger had a fingerprint above it, all the marks of the DSU member.

Out of curiosity, she left her ship and found a spot against the front of her old docking slip to lean and watch the unloading of the DSU ship. What interested her was the fact that the unloading process was smooth and without problems.

The long DSU ship had more to unload at this station than her ship, but several of its workers were in and out of the bay and overseeing the haulers as containers moved out to the wide dock area. It was efficient and without problems, but there was something more. The ship's personnel were having fun. They would poke fun at each other and laugh if anyone had a problem. They helped each other and made jokes out of the work.

Then one of the men grabbed a woman. She laughed and

turned, and before there was any change among the others, they were embracing, deeply kissing. Everyone else ignored the passionate pair, and the work continued. Finally, someone said something and bumped into the couple wrapped around each other. The couple broke apart when some comments were made that caused some prolonged, loud laughter, even from the dockworkers.

"The fellow worker said they could fuck after all the work is done."

As usual, Blu was up against her without any warning.

"So you have superhuman hearing as well as all those muscles." Kina made the statement with a snide whisper. She was trapped between him and the railing where she'd chosen to watch the DSU people.

"No, it is what I would have said to them."

With him being so tall, his chin was above her head. Kina was a tall woman who measured five foot ten inches, but he was about six foot five inches. Her two previous lovers, one in the military, had both been close to her height, and it made her feel strange to realize she would always have to look up at him when they stood together to talk.

"Blu Tho'Drik, this is my last trip for Shayde Freight. I won't miss them, and I sure as hell won't miss having you dog my steps on different stops. Then this is a goodbye for us." She twisted and faced his big chest, forcing herself to look up at his face.

There was a deep frown on his face. "So, you want to be free?" He was looking over at the DSU ship and the people working to unload cartons. "Like everything in life, there is sometimes a heavy price for freedom. Those people over there, they face dangers on their own each time they take the ship they own out to a new destination, every time they take on a contract and wait for the last payment. They share the risks and the profit, what there is, and they help each other face enemies."

Pivoting her head enough to see the nose with the red hand, Kina then looked back and up at his unusual eyes. "Are you free, or are you under contract to a corporation?" Kina was still looking for answers, even though she felt they might be parting.

"You are a fuckin' smart ass for such a beautiful woman. Well, I'm as free as each of my contracts allows me to be. This contract has some pretty tight reins attached to it and keeps me very busy. But I guarantee it is not with a corporation. That is what you were trying to find out, so that information deserves a good kiss." He was lowering his head as if he was going to collect the award.

At the last second, she turned her head, and warm lips were on her cheek. He drew back and laughed. "I'll remember that and collect another time."

In his way that always surprised her, he quietly stepped away and moved quickly among the traffic to disappear. How did such a large male manage to blend into the crowd and not be seen so quickly? It was the first thought in her mind. The second one was that he must be wrong and would not collect the kiss, as they probably would not meet again.

The rest of the deliveries and the return trip were normal, and for the quiet crew, it was boring, but without the camaraderie that had built up over the previous time together. It wasn't as if there was a problem or a falling out with the trio. It seemed as if they all had deep thoughts that kept them all in their cabins or alone.

First, she received an acceptance of her letter of resignation. Of course, it also had a long list of charges that would be deducted from her last bonus, with an itemized detail attached. Shaking her head, she smiled and had no thought of protesting the final charges. As a precaution, she immediately transferred the final amount in her Shayde Freight account to another bank. She requested that her items in the hotel be packed and put in storage and paid the fee for the service and storage, with instructions that she would pick the container up at a later time.

Once they reached the landing zone ground and the back ramp was open, they were met by a security guard contingent that checked the crew out as they left the freighter. This was not normal, but Kina knew it was because the captain was now no longer an employee of the corporation. They would take no chance of her doing any damage to the ship or the AI. A small hauler was following the three as they walked away from the ship.

As the security squad took possession of the *Eclipse,* no transportation was provided for the crew. Kina felt sorry for her two friends, but there was no conversation as they all began to walk across the flat area in the late afternoon. What caught the attention of all three of them as they made their way through some parked ships that did not belong to Shayde was a shrill whistle.

First, they all glanced at the small hauler that was following them. Kina had decided that the security people had assigned the hauler to make sure they left with no problems. It was probably sending back their movements on camera. But when the high-pitched sound came again, they all looked over to see a large man hunched down on the ramp of a ship.

Looking at the small, interesting freighter, all three began to finish each other's sentences.

"Damn, that's the guy that's…" Deak stopped.

"My stalker, who shouldn't even be here on…" Kina's words were almost a whisper.

"On Salcap, but he sure is sitting on a nice ship." Briget, of course, would be the one to see the ship as more important than Blu.

Together, the three people and the small hauler slowly

approached the ship, which had its back open. The long ramp was down to the ground, and Blu was down on a knee.

"You guys look like you need a ride off this bastard corporate planet."

He was casually drawing circles in the dirt with something that might be a straw or stick. Kina had to wonder if it was one of his unusual tech gadgets.

"Well, I was going to head over to the side office to see about getting a ticket on anything that is leaving soon. I'll have to order my carton in storage to be sent over. Does the captain of this ship take on passengers?" Kina recognized the unusually small ship was probably a freighter that could travel very fast in normal space.

"Funny, this one is for sale and needs a damn good crew." Blu looked up at the people in front of him. "Oh, look, there is a whole crew out of work right in front of this ass-end ramp."

"Blu, I'm the only one who put in my resignation." Kina started to step to the side but was stopped by the two people behind her.

"Boss," Deak said in a soft voice. "When Mark One showed us your resignation, we put ours in also. We're both tired of working for others that get rich off of us. Briget and I talked it over and thought we would sit down with you and decide what the future would hold."

Standing and looking around for the first time, Kina was not sure what the future held. But there was one more surprise.

Chapter Twenty

"I'm going with you also, Captain."

It was a voice coming from the little hauler. Mark One, or the AI, was inside the small machine that had been following them.

"What the hell?" or similar words came out of all their mouths, even the big guy, as he stood up to look at the independently moving machine.

"I had drones pull my core and place it in here." A door popped open on the front of the machine, and a complex mix of wires, computer parts, and a glow from some type of electronics was revealed inside.

Turning from the distraction of the AI, Kina looked first at Blu and then inside the ship. It was a large bay suitable for hauling shipments. Ignoring the shock of her friends' statements and the AI, she stepped back to get a better look at the small freighter. Was it possible that some of her problems could be solved this fast?

If this ship was for sale, where was the owner or agent? The late sun let her get a good view of the freighter that was of a decent size. Of course it wasn't huge like *Eclipse,* but it was shaped to handle a reasonable load of cartons and supplies.

Sticking out in the back was a divider lift that had a multitude of uses and divided the two main bays. The back of the ship was flat to allow easy access to each bay, and it flared inward to great round wings that lay on each side, waiting to be filled. There was even a sector in the center that was taller, which would allow for unusual equipment to stand upright or cartons to be stacked higher. From there, the front half of the ship was smooth and extended out to a smaller round nose. From looking at it standing on the crete of the landing area, she would guess that there were cabins in the wider part of the front, and the bridge was supported by the dark glass on top.

What she could see were a lot of different lights, and also what would be panels for sensors and possibly some weapons. All of that would have to be checked out once she was inside. The engines seemed to be larger than expected and were built on as part of the wide flanges on the sides. That would be good for control and steering, and if they were activated, the ship would be fast.

Walking back to where the group was still examining the AI, Kina decided she liked the ship, but it was probably out of her price range. Besides, these types of offers didn't drop into your lap on the very day that you ended your job and needed a new life. It didn't work that way.

What Kina did was walk over to the edge of the ramp where Blu had been kneeling and drawing. She dropped down on her rump, spread her feet, and began to draw circles in the dirt that mimicked his. Her actions slowly drew attention, and everyone got quiet.

At last, Kina spoke. "I'm sorry you guys followed my actions. I had my reasons for going out on my own. Yes, I'm going to get a ticket off this corporate world and then talk to some sales agents and try to find a small ship. I have to start small, and hopefully over time I'll build up to something like the freighter behind me."

A large hand reached down and drew a line through the circles she was making. "Or you could make a down payment on this ship and get a loan to pay off over time from an honest, reputable lender."

It was Blu, down on one heel, too close for her to feel

comfortable. Part of her problem now with the big man was she felt she was fighting some type of attraction to him. She decided that it was impossible for her to like him in any manner, as he was precisely the opposite of what she looked for in a partner. She had always chosen to stay with men who were gentler and more agreed with her opinions and her choices.

This big bully with a foul mouth was rude and aggressive and would not fit into her world. She could not imagine him on a fancy passenger ship or one of the pleasure resorts. No, he would choose a hunt up into a mountain. Well, a trip up to a mountain did sound interesting. *Damn.*

"The agent is available on the main comm unit at the bridge." Blu nodded towards the interior of the ship.

"I could help with the down payment, Boss. That way, I could be a small partner. I'll go in and check out the details." Deak walked past her and moved up the ramp.

"Hey, that's a good idea," added Briget. "I can also put a little into the down payment, and maybe, in case things come together, I think I will go check out the engines on this nice little freighter." Like Deak, Briget walked up the ramp and was gone from sight.

"Captain…" The little hauler rolled up close to the two people left at the edge of the ramp. "May I please enter the ship?"

Raising her face to look him in those beautiful eyes, she shook her head. "You are getting everyone's hopes up for something that might not work out. Damn, I hate you, but okay. I'll go to the bridge and talk to the agent. And Mark, you can enter the ship."

It didn't take long to go through the bay and make her way to climb one of the ladders up to the main level of the ship. From there, it was a clear way through narrow passageways. Finally, the halls merged. Going past a large galley, the last short ramp led up to the bridge. The standard door lock for safety was at the entrance, and Kina stopped to look around.

It was a small, efficient room set up to be run by one or two people. Yet it could hold several more with a couple of extra seats at the curved front dashboard and what looked like pull-down chairs at the back wall.

"If you bring up the main communication setup, there will be a contact open to an office on a different system. You will be put through to the agent with whom you can talk about this ship." Blu was right behind her in his usual quiet manner.

Going over to the pilot's seat, she sat down and waited while the chair comfortably adjusted to her. Sitting there, she could look out through the slanted clear metal that made a window over the dashboard and see beyond the smooth round nose of the ship. Reaching her arms out, she got a feel of the items on the automatic board to see how convenient everything would be for the pilot. It was an expedient setup, better than most, and more advantageous than the *Eclipse.* More information could be drawn up by the mental request of the person sitting in the chair with the right headset.

Perhaps she was being delayed following the big guy's instructions. She knew this would turn out to be a farce, as life was full of disappointments. Not wanting to put the truth off any longer, Kina clicked on the main communication switch. Immediately a free-floating screen became active, which allowed her to see the dashboard through it, but also control its activity.

A logo was displayed that said *Advant Agents. Hit key 255 for Contact.* Using the floating keys on the bottom of the screen, with one finger, Kina tapped in 255.

Within seconds, the screen cleared to a solid form, and a young man in a business setting appeared. "Welcome to the Advant Agency. Well, I see you typed in two five five, so am I addressing Captain Kina Russel?"

Straightening up in the chair, Kina at least wanted to put

on a respectful image. "Yes, this is Captain Russel."

"Good, you are in luck. We are in a different time zone, but…" the handsome young man's eyes wandered to another screen. "I have a flag that if you contacted in, I was to put you directly through to one of our special representatives. One moment, please."

The original logo came back up with some nameless slow music playing, but it was only a moment until a man appeared on the screen. He appeared to be middle age, but with all the tools available, it was hard to guess his age.

"Captain Russel. It is a pleasure to meet you. I am Gal Rehfield, a senior agent at Advant. You have a sponsor, so we do not have to go through all the preliminaries of getting the representation for closing on a sale. Have you had a chance to look over the special freighter and its logs?"

"Actually…" Kina cleared her throat. "Things are moving a little fast for me, and I have only had a few moments to see the ship."

"Well, we must get this deal done as soon as possible." The man spoke sincerely, not like the usual salesman. "At this time, with a loan in place by the DSU, there is a very reasonable down payment that will not last. It is a one-time offer for you only, Captain Russel."

Over her shoulder, a large hand pushed a button on the dash and a note that the logs were available for review appeared.

"Uh, Agent Rehfield, I have the logs to review, and I need to talk to the rest of my crew. Give me some time."

Kina was beginning to have a headache, something that she was never plagued with, even under the pressure of a pilot.

"Well, Captain, again, I need to talk about the urgency. Can you get back to me within two hours' ship time?" The businessman was frowning and also doing something that she could not see.

"Yes. Thank you." The screen now showed the Agency logo again, and Kina swung around in the seat to face the big guy who was still making her life miserable.

"Now, you big asshole, I'm going to get up and walk off this ship and find a way off this planet on another ship unless you start answering questions." All the years of frustration and anger were in her words, and she meant what she was saying.

Looking at her for only a moment, Blu moved back to lean against the rear wall. "I was hired by the person whom the agent referred to as your sponsor. I can't tell you much about him, as it is his right to introduce himself. He is extremely wealthy and has helped a great many people, choosing to help individuals instead of charities or groups."

With a deep sigh that was out of character for him, Blu continued. "I have been known for a long time as a hired gun. Believe it or not, I have some rules, and I'm not going to go into those at this time. He contacted me to be your shepherd and keep you safe. I wasn't sure what that entailed until I started following you and discovered how often you stuck that pretty neck out into dangerous places. It turned out I earned my fee."

He gave her a weak smile. "I get my bonus. If you buy this ship, I come along with it. I get to rub up against that fine body every time we pass in the small hallways."

At that moment, before she could call him words that were not ladylike, Deak stuck his head in the door. "Wow, look at this bridge. Boss, you should see the rest of the ship. It has loading tools that have only been out this last year."

Deak made a fast couple of steps past Blu and jumped into the second seat next to Kina. "I checked out one cabin, and they had a cleansing room, and there are weapons, many weapons, on the outside. We can hold out against almost anyone." His enthusiasm was overflowing, and he wasn't paying any attention that no one was answering his comments.

Hitting a couple of buttons on the dash in front of him, Deak spoke into a comm. "Hey Briget, I'm on the bridge now. Can you hear me?"

"Damn it, Deak. I told you not to bother me. I'm in love and need some time alone with these engines so I can have some Dreamtime. Out." Briget sounded strange, not her usual loud and sharp words.

"Okay, everyone, be quiet and give me some time with these logs." Kina pulled up the electronic version of the ship's records and began to get her head into history. Up to this time, the ship had been called *Perspect*. She knew that if they bought it, they would change the name. That would be interesting. What would she call her first ship?

Chapter Twenty-One

Liber One. It was not a long name to spell, but it was the right name that Captain Russel and her crew christened with the traditional bottle of booze broken on its nose. The action was done right before the crew left the corporate landing zone for the last time.

It had taken Kina an hour to read enough of the log to see that the ship had traveled to long jumps and interesting places. More important, it had been pampered, and its engines added an edge to a larger power. The bays had been treated with expensive spray on metal that gave the promise of added strength to handle any load that was contracted. In other words, according to the log, the ship had not only been treated like a new ship, but it was also better than some that were just off the construction docks.

Kina had left her seat, and with Deak and Blu trailing behind her as captain, she'd spent the next hour inspecting the freighter. She opened every door, each cabinet, and stuck her head inside every panel that she could get opened. She pulled things out and left them lying in the cabins, hallways, and across the floors. She smelled the air in cabins and closets. Some were fresh, and some were strange.

Walking on panels, she'd stomped her feet, and in the large bays, she checked the tie-down locks and banged metal belts against the walls. She stopped at the main engineering section and demanded a report from Briget. Here was the odor of heat and oil, and success.

The woman had dust and grease on her ship suit and a

smile a mile wide on her face as she gave a detailed description of the power of the two main space engines and the size of the jump core engine. At last, Kina had ended up in the galley, made no comment to the fact that coffee was ready, but poured herself a large mug full.

With coffee in hand and her followers in tow, she'd finally returned to the bridge to sit in the pilot's chair.

With a sigh and a sip of the coffee, she had at last punched in the 255 and waited for Agent Rehfield. "Now we get the bad news." Those were her soft words while she waited for the representative. The talk about the price was exhausting, with both Deak and Briget bringing in snacks and drinks. Mostly, they reminded Kina of how much they could contribute and cheered her up.

The overall price was a shock to all of them. It was high because the freighter was in such good condition. But there was a way to get the down payment lower and the regular payments in various amounts.

What Kina was trying to consider was whether they could obtain the ship, meet the loan payments, and have some reserve funds for travel and investments as they contracted for loads.

But then Agent Rehfield had a surprise. He had a shipment that needed to be picked up on a moon that was in the central system and needed to be rushed out to a very long group of jumps. It had a payment upfront and a bonus if the delivery arrived on time. It was waiting for a pickup.

Finally, the Agent stated that a decision had to be made immediately, and Blu stepped forward and laid an item on the dashboard in front of Kina and Deak. It was a hand weapon—a special one with a glow reflected from the dials that announced it was made from an extraordinary metal.

"My share," Blu announced and then stepped back. This was the only thing he had said through the long afternoon and evening as Kina talked business with the Agent. The only thing that did not glow with a silver polish was a small amount of leather grip on both sides of the handle. It was heavy and made a loud sound when the big hand released it onto the flat area.

The Agent was waiting for an answer, but Kina and Deak were looking at the unusual handgun, trying to decide what they were looking at and how dangerous it was lying there.

Suddenly Deak hit a drawer below the place where he sat. It opened and held several tools. He pulled one out that was similar to a scanner and held it over the gun. With a beep, he got a readout that he held over for Kina to read.

"It is made of Rhodium. That is worth a lot." Kina glanced up at where Blu was again, leaning against the back wall. He only did one nod and remained like a large statue.

"Boss." Deak reached over and muted the screen, so the Agent didn't hear them. "The current price of Rhodium is about fourteen thousand one hundred an ounce in funds. That thing is light and weighs about eighteen ounces. So its value on the rare metal market would be between two hundred and fifty and two hundred and sixty thousand."

They'd both sat for a moment and stared at the hunk of metal in an unusual shape, and then Kina hit the speaker mode. "Agent, we will take your third choice. Send the forms through, and they will be signed immediately. I will send the first down payment back with the papers. Also, please send us the contract for the first delivery."

It was in the galley where they met after Briget transferred Mark One's core into the bridge's special slot and two other control areas. She and Deak took the AI from the freighter they had just purchased, put it in the small hauler, and sent it back to the *Eclipse*.

Now was their time to name their ship and their group to be registered members of the Democratic Shippers Universal.

It was their first intention to join and pay dues to that organization.

"What do we name the ship?" It was Briget who asked the important question, but it was on all of their minds as they sat and looked down at the table or the floor.

"You are all free now. Maybe that is a good word," Blu said from the area where he was filling his mug with coffee.

"But you can't call a ship *Free*. That sounds a bit strange." Briget frowned as she added her thoughts.

Working on her pad, Kina held it up. "In an ancient Earth language, Free is also Liber. We could call it *Liber One* for our first venture together."

The vote was quick and unanimous. Their ship had a name.

"You know, *Liber One* means our goal. But what are we as a team or company together on this ship?" Deak was getting drunk but was still adding to the conversation.

"I am not human and have never been in the field, but if you are hunting and are free, what do you do next?" Mark One was part of the discussion.

Both Deak as a weapons expert and Blu answered together. "Aim."

"Yes!" Kina slammed her hand on the table. "We are Aim, Incorporated." So now the ship had a name, and the group had a title. They were ready for business and really in trouble.

It was agreed by everyone that Kina was the head of their company, and even though they all had equal votes, she would have the right to veto any item. This was an easy choice, since Captain Russel had the most funds invested and had been offered the freighter at the beginning.

The first contact they had with Shayde Security as they were firing up the engines to leave Salcap, was a complaint about problems with the AI on Eclipse. Deciding to ignore the persistent comm notices from the officials and knowing that they would not get a clean release, as soon as Briget gave the okay, Kina took them straight up and then on a fast outward circle to leave.

Deak had to take over the speakers and alarms as they got calls from angry ships, controllers, and anyone else that seemed upset with ships moving too fast. Kina was surprised and pleased at the handling of a ship of this size as the engines responded to her while she threaded through the traffic around the busy planet.

Using the hand control that was on the dashboard in easy reach allowed her to have the other hand free to make adjustments with the small side jets. Steering with the round nose was like driving a small vehicle, and the smooth shape of the freighter moved in directions the big boxy *Eclipse* could not make. Kina even had a slight smile on her face as the shape and the somewhat smooth spaceship was made to move through traffic and, even better, would handle the shapes in the asteroid belts.

Within an hour, the *Liber One* was beyond the traffic around the heavily civilized world. In another two hours, they had reached a jump point, and Deak was giving Mark One the first navigation points to take them for their first pickup.

With the first jump under their belts, and the need to travel fast but just under light speed in regular space, the crew was now ready to settle into their ship.

"First, we need to clean up and check the corners," Kina announced through the ship's speaker system. Deak agreed, then got up, went to the sidewall, and opened the cabinets. Everything had been opened at least once, but this time he began to pull articles out onto the metal floor.

Following his example, Kina went to the opposite wall and did the same thing to the tall closet. To her surprise, it was full of weapons.

"Blu," Kina called out loudly. She had discovered that he

was never very far away from her.

The big man stuck his head in the door from the hall and looked at her, standing over her pile of weapons.

"Can you check these out?"

"Done." Blu entered the bridge to come over to the small space to where she was standing.

Feeling all of her unusual emotions, from anger to something else she would not admit, she gave him a push and stepped around him to leave the area and go out through the narrow hallway. She was still not sure she trusted him, even though he had helped her purchase the freighter. The dusty, dirty group broke for lunch and found Briget cleaning out the galley. But Briget did find time to prepare sandwiches and brought out cold juice for everyone.

It was back to work, with breaks in between and everyone needing a shower before supper. By the end of the day, they had hardly touched the front of the ship and had set their schedule for the next few weeks as they took the jumps and then spent weeks in normal space.

The ship had not been deeply inspected and cleaned by the time they reached the point where they were to pick up the load for their first shipment.

The location was in a sparsely settled manufacturing world called Mayall, which had only two landing zones. The controller made contact with them when they came into the area of the three small moons that circled the planet.

"This is Mayall Control. State your business or move on. Over."

Looking over at Deak, Kina raised an eyebrow. "Not too friendly." She then spoke to Mark One. "Mark, please put me through to the controller."

"Acknowledged. General mic." Mark had been using a very nice young male voice since running on *Liber*.

"Hello, Mayall Control. This is freighter *Liber One*. We have a contract to obtain some items to ship from a company called Pendent. Can you confirm which is the correct landing zone for us to reach that company/. Over?"

"Mayall Control to freighter Liber One. Welcome. You will need to sit down on the northern landing zone known as Counties Homebound. I'm sending you the coordinates. And, uh, good luck. Out."

"Well, that was unusual, Boss. He didn't sound like he was wishing us good luck in the way most people do. I wonder what we have run into on our first trip?" Deak was bringing up the view of the world as they came in closer and were getting an idea of the topography.

It was a rough world, broken up with rocky terrain and mountains everywhere. That meant the ores were near the surface and were the backbone of the industry the planet had developed.

Coming out of orbit and into the lower atmosphere, it was easy to find the landing zone for any spaceship. To begin with, there wasn't much air traffic, but a lot of large land crawlers, some several miles long. The flat landing area had lots of high buildings that looked like manufacturing or commercial in nature on one side and a cliff on another. The rest was just land that looked like it had been misused, with deep ruts and tracks.

There was one small ship that looked like something with weapons on it but with many mismatched parts on its sides, that sat by itself. Near the buildings was a freighter that was being loaded. But the activity was slow.

"This doesn't look good," Kina was speaking to herself, but out loud.

"Good instinct, beauty. Park us far away and let them work to bring us the containers. I'll go out first and look around."

No one argued with Blu's suggestion.

Chapter Twenty-Two

They did draw attention when they landed. Several land vehicles began to move towards the *Liber One* almost before the engines had stopped.

"Let me go out first." Blu's voice sounded gruff as he started back to the rear of the ship.

"I'll go with him." Deak jumped up and was soon following through to the back, where a smaller ramp was lowered out of the bay. On the way, Blu grabbed a long gun. He already had a pistol on his hip. Taking the lead of the big guy, Deak grabbed a large, long gun that took two hands to carry.

When the vehicles stopped and men came out of each, on her screen, Kina saw that they all hesitated when they saw the prominent figure of Blu on the end of the ramp. Was it the weapons or the big figure that caused the people to stop and wait?

With his voice loud enough to carry to everyone, Blu stayed on the edge of the ramp and called out, "Anyone here represent the Pendent Company?"

With those words, Deak pulled his big weapon around, and in the light of the bay, he was seen at the top of the ramp. The two made an impressive duo for her ship's security. After a moment of hesitation, some people began to get back into their vehicles, and a couple of them slowly walked towards the ramp. They had their hand up about chest high, and when they got close, one held a hand out to shake.

There were some small words that Kina could not hear that Blu said over his shoulder to Deak as he stepped forward.

"Before we touch palms, how about you send IDs over to my ship's AI so we can confirm whom we are talking with?"

"Oh, of course. Very rude of me, here." The man held up a pad and hit a couple of keys.

"Mark, are you getting anything?" Kina watched a second small screen on her dashboard as the AI worked some receiving electronics.

"Confirmed, Captain. It seems the man does represent Pendent. It would now be prudent to find where the items we are supposed to ship are located?" The AI that was becoming sentient added an excellent suggestion.

Sending a silent green light to Blu's and Deak's wrist comm let the two men know that the guy's ID checked out to be for the company her crew needed to contact.

The big guy was looming over the guy from Pendent and speaking in his usual harsh voice. "Okay, my friend back there is going to keep his famous gun ready in case anything goes differently than what I want. Where are the cartons we are to pick up? We are short on time and not here to make friends, only to do a good job. What happens next could affect your health."

Shaking her head, Kina had to agree. Blu was not going to make friends with that attitude. On the other hand, as Mark used a tiny drone no larger than a bug and began to move in and fly over the others that had gotten out of the vehicle, there was a surprise. Two that had departed from the other side had long guns up and aimed over the top of the roof. *Damn.* Blu had good instincts, and this was not a friendly group.

"Mark, bring out a weapon drone and send it out over that vehicle." Giving the order to protect her people seemed like going to war for Kina.

"I already have one ready. I'm sending it out now. I have the view from it on your split screen."

Kina couldn't help but notice that Mark did sound a little

smug.

"I think you should light up the guys behind the vehicle to give our men the information and surprise the guy talking to Blu." Kina expanded the side of the screen with the land vehicle. She sent a yellow light to the two men's wrist comm to warn them before the drone got into place.

The light was bright, and a broad circle surrounded the vehicle, showing two men and their long guns. The light surprised them and, for a moment, blinded them, and they ducked, one man losing his weapon. Then they finally stood and looked over at the two on the other side of the transport. All four of them mumbled between themselves and then looked at the guy standing in front of Blu, who was pointing his gun into that man's chest.

"Make sure I can hear what Blu and the Pendent rep are saying, Mark."

"Confirmed." With that, the voices were coming in clear.

"We came to pick up some cartons, but we don't mind blowing up a unit and leaving some bodies. When is someone going to bring out the cartons we were sent here to pick up?" Blu was shoving the long gun into the man so hard that the man had to take a step or two back.

"Sir, easy. This is just a misunderstanding. We might have thought you were marauders and that we needed to attack and acquire a ship through the right of possession. We did not expect you for another few days. I apologize. If you give us some time, we can begin to have the containers moved over and loaded on board your ship." The man was talking too fast and looking around, perhaps for help from his men. They were not about to do anything with an armed drone and its light holding them hostage.

"Now, sir." The man tried to step back again.

Blu placed his large hand on the man's shoulder.

"Sir, I was going to suggest that I leave and arrange for

your shipment."

"I don't think that will work. Use your pad to arrange for the shipment to come out immediately. You and your friends will wait right here until everything gets loaded. That way, you and I will be really satisfied with a job that is done the right way." With one hand preventing the man from moving, Blu nudged him again with the weapon.

"Mark, send out two more weapons drones to protect our crew." Kina now had the scene of the back ramp up on the large screen overhead. She leaned back, worried about her two men.

"Confirmed, Captain."

The AI must have anticipated her wishes, as suddenly there were more lights over the area and a burst of one shot at a man behind the vehicle who had turned to move his weapon.

Pushing the rep man to his knees, Blu spoke loud enough for all to hear. "I think you are outgunned. You'd better hope that the shipment reaches here before my captain loses her patience. She is a very anxious female."

As Kina watched the clock, time seemed to come to a standstill. On the upper part of the ramp, Deak was now sitting and using his drawn-up knees to rest and allow the big gun to aim at the vehicle and four men. Blu was standing with his legs a bit apart, looking like a statue that could be in that position for hours. He had one hand on the shoulder of the kneeling man, and the other held his pistol on the man's head with the long gun now over his back.

It was over an hour later when Mark drew her attention to the motion at the side of the flat landing area. The AI brought up another screen from a camera on that side of the ship. It showed a long train of auto haulers coming towards them.

No one moved, but Mark sent one of the drones to fly over

the lead hauler and let them see it in the circle of white light. The light reflected off the hauler and stayed with it as it slowly crossed the area. At last, the long train without any human driver came to a halt almost at the heels of the kneeling man in front of Blu.

Blu did not move or shift. He stood solidly with his handgun on the rep and then announced in a low voice, "This gentleman is going to go with me aboard our ship. He is going to wait to make sure the rest of you oversee the transfer of the containers from the hauler to our bay. When everything is finished, all of you can go to the nearest bar and get a strong drink."

With his great strength, Blu picked up the man. He held him high up, the toes of his shoes barely touching the metal of the ramp as they went backward. They stepped off to a side, leaving Deak with a clear view for the weapon he held steadily trained on the vehicle.

The drones seemed to move a little lower, but the light still flooded the area for everything to be seen. The men didn't have to contribute much when it came to loading the containers. Bridget was soon out in full armor, checking each unit as it was set into position. She kept her eyes open as some were stacked on others, but didn't change anything at this time, saving that for later if needed.

The big guy was still a statue with the rep down on the metal floor at his feet and the pistol pointed at his head. But if one looked closely at Blu, his eyes were moving—never missing anything. At last, the final container was in place, and Briget began to start connecting the tie-downs.

"Captain, can I release the rep? Is everything a go now?" Blu announced loudly, depending on the AI to pick up his voice and let Kina hear on the bridge.

Taking a moment to check the paperwork and that the first portion of the payment was received, Kina could now relax.

"Security, you are relieved of duty. Move all non-ship personnel from the ship, as we are going to lock down for takeoff."

Checking the information the dashboard gave her about the ship, Kina watched as Blu roughly helped the rep down the ramp. The man had hardly got to his feet and away from the edge of the metal ramp when it began to pull upward to seal the back of *Liber One*. They were leaving this pick-up point and would not miss it. On her screen, she could see both men helping Briget finish the tie-downs and checking everything in the bay.

"Mark, take us out into the system safely but as fast as possible. We have a couple of long jumps to deliver this load."

"Confirmed, Captain."

The AI was capable of taking over the navigation system, as Kina had already put in the astrogation figures needed. Now she needed to meet the crew in the galley and talk about the problems at the landing zone.

Chapter Twenty-Three

Being the first at the table was rare for Kina, so she didn't sit down. She opened the cold chest and pulled out water and juices to put on the table. Next, she grabbed some trays Briget had prepared full of fruit, meat slices, and cheese. By the time she turned around for the last time, the crew was finally coming through the wide door of the galley.

The galley was one of the areas on the ship that did not have a door lock to close or support anyone. It was just a wide opening on that side of a narrow hall that was almost the size of the room itself. Most of the room was open to allow more people than this small crew to be served at the table or work at the counters. On the other hand, the ship was efficient and could be run properly by the small number of people on it at this time.

There was silence as the four people found seats and something to chug down. It seemed the whole mess out on the landing site was so strange that none of them had anything to discuss.

"Does that happen to independent shippers very often?" Kina asked as she looked over at Blu.

"I think that was a mistake. They thought they could take advantage of someone new on their location." Blu sat back and stared at her, looked first at her eyes, and then began to let his focus move downward.

Heat came to Kina's cheeks.

Briget stuffed some food in her mouth and talked around it. "It seems that it is good to have a big security guy on an indie ship." No one disagreed.

After the first jump and a long journey through normal space, they all split up, with Mark watching for other ships and making sure the ship stayed on course. Briget had a small room set up in one of the engines' alcoves. Deak had found an area near the top of the ship where the extra controls for outside weapons were handled and also had a bunk. He settled down there and was happy.

A large storage closet next to the armory was available, and Blu soon converted it into his cabin. Included was a full bathroom for common use across the narrow hall, and low metal shelving was quickly converted into a bunk. A plain dark metal room with some hooks and shelves suited him fine.

Two cabins were behind the bridge and across from the galley. Kina took the first one, and they all joked that the second one would be for paying passengers. For a freighter, it was plain but comfortable. The built-in bunk was wider than average, and there were a couple of tall cabinets with solid doors. It had a small private bath, and the room included a table, a couple of pull-down chairs, and full contact with the entire ship.

The AI could now watch over all the crew and also the ship in limited zones of control on the power and direction. So the bored team found movies and vids, did exercises, and ate together. One of the rooms had games, including poker, that Deak always seemed to win.

"Before we deliver the cartons, Deak will own the ship," Briget complained as she threw her chips into the pot.

Fortunately, before another game could be dealt, Mark announced over the speaker system that they were going through the last jump.

At last, they were busy and energetic. Kina took her pilot's seat to be captain again. Briget was in the bay to oversee the unhooking of the containers. The security crew was armed and ready to be the first ones down the ramp in their usual rehearsed position. But fortunately, this time, things were different.

First, there was only one spaceship landing zone, and there was a controller in charge. The contact went smoothly and professionally after Captain Russel gave the ship's ID and a request to land to deliver their load to the other end of Pendent Company.

A ground crew directed them where to park the ship. Before they had the ship's engines all shut down, haulers were coming out of a large storage building with a small land vehicle that had the flag announcing Pendent Company on the front fender. Working people were everywhere, most with reflective colors to prove some safety regulations.

A man and a woman got out of the land vehicle that had pulled over to one side, and the lady stepped forward with a large pad.

"Welcome, *Liber One*. We understand you have our shipment. Can we check it on your ship before starting to unload, if that is acceptable?" The lady spoke in a friendly manner, and the man behind her nodded and smiled.

Blu looked around, and with his sharp eyes, he saw no weapons anywhere. "One moment so that I can get clearance from my captain." He did not move, but he lifted his hand holding the weapon that also had a wrist comm. He spoke into it even though he knew Kina was watching and listening from the ship's cameras. "Captain, permission to allow the client to inspect their containers."

Hitting a button that would allow her words to be heard at the ramp entrance, Kina smiled. "Permission granted for the main bay only."

"Copy, Captain." For the first time, Blu lowered his gun, relaxed his stance, and stepped aside. "There is one crew inside by the cartons that can assist you. Please enter." Blu decided it might not hurt to be polite in return to the lady.

Deak didn't move, but he did let the big gun slide down to the metal floor between his feet and knees. He would stay in the sitting position to watch the progress and work out on the landing area.

The couple acknowledged Briget and began to check each carton. They did not touch or ask to open anything. They did check the seals and then the numbers against their manifest. They were efficient but complete and soon had looked at every carton.

The lady turned back to the ramp exit and spoke to Blu, evidently not put off by his threatening size.

"Sir, let your captain know we appreciate her good work, and it would be a pleasure to use the service of *Liber One* again. I am transferring the rest of the funds right now." She then hit some keys on the large pad.

The captain's voice came through on an overhead speaker. "Thank you, madam. The funds have cleared. Do you need help with the unloading?"

The woman looked over at the man, and from his negative nod, she answered. She glanced up at the speaker. "We have enough help as long as the ship's tie-downs have been released."

The unloading went without a problem, and even Deak finally moved out of the way, putting the big gun away. Few people came on board, as the small haulers were efficient and ran with limited AIs. The little movers loaded themselves onto the final of the big trailers, along with the last containers.

The fancy land vehicle with the flag was long gone, but as the last of the haulers were starting to pull away, another more military-style vehicle pulled up. Two men stepped out and sat two boxes at the bottom of the ramp.

"Compliments of Pendent and Mrs. Galaut. Enjoy." The men threw a rough salute and left.

Always one to be wary of gifts in sealed packages, Blu ran a deep scanner over the boxes to find one full of special frozen meat and the other holding six bottles of some type of alcohol, probably whiskey from the fancy label. A note was attached for the captain.

With the ship sealed up but still on the landing zone, they all met in the galley to enjoy the gift and find out what the note was to the captain. It was a notice that if they could wait for two days, Pendent had a small container that needed to be rushed to a nearby moon. They would pay double the rate for the inconvenience of the delay.

It was a long trip through normal space without a jump needed.

"Well?" Kina was calling for a vote. "We have one bad experience with this company and one good one. We also got paid per the contract. Do we take this new one with them?"

The discussion was a battle of opinions, but it all boiled down to the fact that an indie ship needed every opportunity offered. So they had the AI send out a contact to the lady at Pendent, and they had a couple of days to relax planet side.

Deak and Kina were negotiating with a local vendor for produce such as food and fruit that would be good supplies for the ship. Unfortunately, the negotiations were turning more into a fight. Kina sighed. It seemed that her life was turning into nothing but fights and war. She had thought that getting away from the control of the corporation would give her freedom. It had led her to more battles.

Leaving Deak to finish the directions to get the produce to the ship, Kina stomped off. She made her way back to the ship, wondering what type of life she had entered. With her head down, Kina was made her way up through the ship's narrow hall. She reached over to punch her palm plate at her cabin at the same time as she ran into a wall.

Throwing his arms around her to keep both of them from

falling, Blu turned them so that there was enough room, as her back was in the doorway. He slowly let go of her as if making sure she was stable on her feet. That moment she looked up at him, and there was something else in those eyes. It was not the usual mockery. She saw almost a question in the depth of those beautiful blue eyes.

Suddenly, Kina decided she was tired of fighting the world, but more important, she was tired of fighting herself. Instead of moving back and away into her cabin, she raised her arms over those broad shoulders and locked her hands around his neck. Then she pulled to encourage him.

It was the answer he must have been looking for as he dipped his head down and their lips met. His kiss was not gentle—it was devouring. She vaguely thought Blu would never do anything less than all the way. His arms around her lifted her from the ground. But to show him that she was also into this all the way, she locked her legs around him, and they were instantly in her cabin together as the door slid closed.

Chapter Twenty-Four

The next day everyone was back on the *Liber One* and waiting for the shipment to arrive. A flat vehicle with the name of Pendent on it, driven by one man, pulled up at the end of the ramp where Blu stood on guard. Deak was relieved to have such a presence always protecting him.

"Delivery for Captain Russel," the man announced as he stepped from the open cab and held out a pad.

Blu checked, signed, and got a notice on his wrist comm from Kina that the first part of the payment had been transferred.

A small hauler containing a crate backed off the loader and moved up into the bay.

"Sir," the driver said politely. "The hauler will go with the carton and stay at the delivery point. Thank you." With that, the man got back in the cab and drove away.

Going up into the bay and closing the ramp exit, Blu waited while Deak and Briget went about tying down their unusual load. It took extra work to get the shape of the little hauler with its small carton tied down to suit Briget. At last, everything seemed in place, and Briget disappeared into one of the engine rooms.

That left Deak and Blu to go up to the bridge to find seats for the lift-off. Deak slid into the second seat at the dashboard and watched Blu and Kina ignore each other. Something had happened between those two, but no one was speaking about any problems, so Deak was not going to poke around. He hoped things would settle down soon. They both did their jobs as well or better than usual. It was only that they did not speak to each other except in short sentences.

Deak shook his head. If things didn't improve between the two most important people on the ship, this was going to be a difficult trip. They had a long journey, in normal space of a couple of weeks, to get to the location to deliver the small package.

What was happening between these two strong personalities was a heavy attraction that they had never faced before. What they did was find a way to spend a few hours in Kina's cabin when no one was around. They made wild love in that room and ended up sweaty in each other's arms. They slowly, after a few nights, began to talk about their past, their childhood, and small bits of gossip. It wasn't much, but it was small bits of their lives that they had never shared with anyone else.

But a problem had developed. They didn't know what to say to each other during regular work hours. In the past, there had been bitter words and teasing. They had exchanged put-downs and snide comments as they ate together or worked alongside each other. They had no words with any meaning to say from either of them. At least nothing could be said in front of the other crewmembers.

Kina had kept all the secrets inside about what she had plotted with the Shayde security in trying to trap her stalker on so many different times. Over time she had been at so many separate docking sites where she had worked with the local law to try and trap the dark figure that was always following her.

The memories of hate for someone unfamiliar had haunted her and left her sleepless and needing to see him in bars or dead. How could she share these recollections with him, or better, how could she erase them and reconcile them with her present feelings?

Blu also had problems in his mind. He still was unable to share with this marvelous female the details of the person who had hired him to protect her. He still had the small, amazing ship that he could call out of the dark space whenever he needed it, and he had not told her that he had the black ship.

Although at this time he did not need to use any of them, he still had hidden away the many tech items she called gadgets—the new products that his benefactor obtained for him or he got among his strange contacts that were often so rare they were still in Research and Development for the military.

They both had the same problem. How did you have open conversations with someone you liked when you had secrets?

At last, the AI announced that they had reached the delivery location. It turned out to be a busy rotation space station that was in orbit over the moon that was being mined for precious ores. As it turned out, this position was near a jump point and a good re-supplying point for a lot of ships.

The station's controller was efficient and professional, and they were assigned a docking point that let them slip in the round nose and about a third of the ship. This put enough of the *Liber One* inside the docking area to unload the shipment through a side exit and put the front in an atmospheric environment.

As usual, Blu went out first to check out the docking area and give approval for safety. Kina watched him look so intimidating as he prowled the part of the ship trapped in the dock. At last he gave a nod, and the bay side exit door lock was opened. Briget stood there waiting for the client to claim the product complete in its little hauler.

Pointing at a screen showing a group of laughing people, Deak commented. "You know, we need to get to know some of those people. After all, we are part of their group now."

He was referring to the fact that some of the people had the small red hand stitched on the left breast of their mismatched ship suits—fellow members of the Democratic Shippers Universal that the *Liber One* was now affiliated with.

"Well." Kina smiled. "You like poker. Get in a game with some of them and make friends. Just don't cheat or take all their funds." At last, she got up from her seat, deciding she would go and join the big guy outside. On her way, she reached Briget on the comm to see if the woman wanted to join them.

"Thanks, Captain, but I am going to get a small part for a side motor, and then in a few hours, I'm going to join Deak. He says he hopes to get some kind of game going." There was banging in the background as Briget spoke. The engineer was always working, and Kina thought she was the best in the business.

After a few hours of shopping, Blu suggested they settle down at an open restaurant and eat a slow meal. Kina contacted Mark, on her wrist comm and requested that it send a drone to pick up the items they had purchased. It could transfer those things back to the ship, leaving her to enjoy her meal.

After the drone picked up their packages and it was getting late, they debated about going back to the ship when they got a comm message from Deak. It was a text saying he was in a game and wanted them to join him with a bunch of DSU members. He gave the location, so the pair took a mover down several floors into a rougher sector of the station.

The bar was dark and smoky, exactly as expected, except

there was laughter and cheering. With no fights or loud complaining, it was a happier association, with everyone having fun and seeming to know each other. It took only a couple of glances from the doorway to see that most of the customers had *red hand* embroidered on their outfits. So, this was a favorite bar for the members of DSU.

Leaning down so he could whisper to her, Blu said a few quiet words. "You go join Deak. I don't play games. Breaking bones are my sport. I'll get us a drink."

Moving through the crush of smiling, drinking people, Kina had spotted Deak with a couple of onlookers hanging over his shoulder. He had a reasonable pile of chips, so he was playing smart, winning some but not everything.

"Ah, here's my boss. Move over, and someone grab her a chair." Deak was giving orders in a loud voice, but it worked, as room was made for her beside him when a chair appeared immediately.

"You're right in time for the next hand. I'll even loan you some chips." Deak slid her some loose chips, and someone across the table began to shuffle the five-sided solid cards. By the time she got all of her cards and put in the ante. Blu reached over her shoulder and placed a small glass with amber liquid in front of her.

"Wow, is that your bodyguard?" A woman on the other side of the table looked up at Blu with a wink.

Kina decided that the woman was flirting with him. "Nope."

Deak laughed out loud. "This is the boss's maid. You should see what the bodyguard looks like." With that, he raised the pot. That brought a lot of laughter from everyone.

Kina looked up at Blu, and he only raised an eyebrow. Okay, he was taking in everything as he looked over the crowd.

"So…" A man next to Kina said to her as he met the raise.

"Your buddy here tells us you are new but don't have your hand yet. We need to change that. We need to let all the pirates and even the Feds or whoever else is out in the dark know. Don't mess with the hand."

Without laughter, there were several *ayes* from around the table. Okay, these people were together, and maybe she did need to belong to the group.

After a couple of hours of drinking and games and good tales about clients who demanded strange agreements, the subject turned.

"So, newbie, have you put the red hand on the nose of your ship yet?" This came from the woman who was introduced as Mato and who was sitting next to Kina.

"Nope, not sure how that works." Kina tipped her glass as she spoke. She had thrown her cards in on the last bid. Blu was providing her with something that was not alcoholic. That was smart, as she wanted to learn from these people. He stood right behind her or sometimes leaned his back against the bar, watching the room.

"Oh, a red hand initiation." This was yelled out by one slightly drunk man at their table and was soon repeated around the room.

"Where's your ship docked?" Mato asked as she stood up and began to pull on Kina's arm. Suddenly she had the big hand of Blu separating them. "Sorry, big guy, no problem. We are going to get you guys into the club. Let's head out to your ship. Where is your crew?"

People began to grab their drinks, and Deak stood and led the way toward the door. Suddenly there was a parade of laughing spacers, some slightly drunk, spilling out into the wide hallway. Kina was in the middle of the chaos with one of Blu's arms around her in a protective manner.

The group must have been thirty-five or forty people, and

they were laughing and raising their drinks to salute others as they made their way to the movers. They were loading as many as possible on each lift as the doors closed, and they went up to the docking level. The doors of the movers opened, one after another, and the happy tipsy crowd re-formed to make their way out to the dock area.

The guard at the side entrance tried to stop them to ask for IDs, and a couple shared their drinks as others crawled over the barriers. Giving into the fun party, the guard opened the doors, and they were in the wide busy loading area. Auto haulers were shifting cartons as the band of happy people pushed Kina and Blu, and Deak over to their ship. It dawned on her that they still had not even found the time to paint the name on *Liber One*.

"Someone find a bucket of clear metal."

Kina wasn't sure who had called out for the product, but there was a lot of shuffling, and then someone ran from another ship, yelling and smiling and holding a battered bucket over his head.

By this time, Briget had come out to stand on the top of the entrance to the door lock as if defending the ship. Suddenly Kina found the front of her ship surrounded in a circle. The laughing company had now pulled back to form a space where only a few were close to the nose of the ship. It was Mato, the ship's crew, and another man.

The man had a canteen, a flat pan that he was now pouring the clear liquid metal into carefully. "We have to work quickly as the metal dries fast. Which of you has the biggest hand?"

Everyone looked at Blu, who stood so close behind Kina.

"Okay, the maid gets to be the hand." When the kneeling man made the half-drunken statement, everyone laughed and saluted him with their almost empty mugs and glasses.

Mato stepped forward. "Here is the process. Each crew member must cut their palm and drip blood into the pan until the clear metal turns the right shade of red. Hurry and step up now."

There was no movement and only the shuffling from the collection of people around them. But Kina decided she wanted this, so she stepped away from Blu to stand above the pan.

"Who has a sharp knife?" Kina hoped someone would give her one. Of course, Blu was the one who pulled a thin blade from somewhere. It was sharp, and she let the blood drip into the clear liquid. While she stood there, Deak approached and took the knife from her to repeat her action. As their blood mixed, she had no idea when Briget moved in, but Kina stepped back and allowed the engineer to do her part. The last one was Blu, and he didn't hesitate. He made the deep cut with his knife, wiped the blade on his pants, and it disappeared in his clothes.

The man on the ground opened the canteen he had and poured water on the ground to make a small pool. "Okay, big guy, place your hand in the water so the metal won't stick to you. Then flatly put your hand into the red metal and stamp it on the nose of your ship."

Even half-drunk, the instructions were clear.

Chapter Twenty-Five

The *Liber One* was out into space hunting for a jump gate. They had ways to go, as there was a dark hole in this system, and the jump places were only available far away from the greedy black destroyed stars.

The crew was in their usual places on board, as they had a new contract. But since they had time, Kina had instructed Mark One to send out a drone bot to paint the name of the ship on the nose and the ID numbers on the tail. She sat in her pilot's seat, watching the process on a screen as she peeled the last traces of small bits of the red metal from the first finger on her right hand. It also matched the finger mark in red above the large red hand on her ship that announced their membership in the DSU.

The weapons on the upper section were being checked out, so Deak was crawling around in strange places on the ship. Briget was lost somewhere in the back or side of the ship, where the engines were working. Briget always needed to be with her babies.

Two large warm hands slowly enclosed Kina's shoulders, and she looked up with a smile. Those beautiful, strange blue eyes were something she felt she would never get tired of seeing. Enjoying the feel of the big male who rarely smiled, Captain Kina Russel of the freighter *Liber One*, a member of the Democratic Shippers Universal, thought about secrets.

The Universe was full of secrets, and some of them were waiting to be discovered, but a few should always be kept close to never be told. The deep dark of space held so much for those who were strong enough to conquer it, but it still was a dangerous place that held life at a price. *Liber One* had a strong crew and a brilliant AI, along with being a good ship. Perhaps there would be a time in the future to discover one secret—who was Kina's benefactor, and why had he chosen her?

The End.